Moti Nandy (1931–2010) was one of the few writers in the world to have created an entire body of fiction centred on sports. A Sahitya Akademi award-winner and former Sports Editor at the *Anandabazar Patrika*, he wrote more than twenty-five novels in Bengali for adults, and as many for children and young adults. Nearly all his novels are set in Kolkata, where he lived, and capture the struggle and success of the underdog in sports, ranging from football to cricket, tennis to swimming, athletics to boxing.

Arunava Sinha translates classic, modern and contemporary Bengali fiction, non-fiction and poetry into English. Over forty of his translations have been published so far. Born and educated in Kolkata, he lives and writes in Delhi.

RIGHT ARM OVER

MOTI NANDY

Translated by ARUNAVA SINHA

talking
CUB

TALKING CUB
Published by Speaking Tiger Publishing Pvt. Ltd
4381/4 Ansari Road, Daryaganj,
New Delhi–110002, India

Copyright © Moti Nandy 1989
Translation copyright © Arunava Sinha 2018

First published in Bengali as *Jibon Ananto* by Ananda
Publishers in 1989
First published in English by Speaking Tiger in paperback 2018

ISBN: 978-93-88070-42-3
eISBN: 978-93-88070-30-0

10 9 8 7 6 5 4 3 2 1

The moral right of the author has been asserted.

Typset in Adobe Garamond Pro by Jojy Philip
Printed at Gopsons Papers Ltd.

1

'Okay, can you guess tomorrow's headlines?'
'I can.'
'What will they say?'
'"Dramatic last ball win for Friends' Society".'
'Lousy headline.'
'Okay then, "Breathless finish to CAB Knockout".'
'Even worse.'
'Okay, let's see…'

Nudging away the boots he had just taken off, Jibon stretched his legs out and glanced at Ananto. 'Sports headlines are like literature these days,' Ananto said, bending over to pull off his sweat-soaked shirt. Easing his arms out of the sleeves, he said, '"Jibon's sixer gives new life to Friends". Or, "Jibon makes Agragami's life miserable".'

'Nothing can be lousier than this "Jibon-life" thing.' Jibon put his feet up on the empty chair in front of him. 'Sounds like kids' adventure stories.'

'I'll tell you the headline after a shower.' Wrapping a towel around his waist, Ananto took his trousers off.

'Wait, me first. So hot! Who plays cricket on a May afternoon in India? Please Antu, let me go first.'

Jibon jumped to his feet. But before he could take a step towards the bathroom, Ananto ran past him to lock himself inside, shouting, 'You know the headline? "Jibon stakes a claim to the Ranji team".'

'What's the use of staking a claim at the end of the season?'

'This performance will count when they select the Bengal team next season,' Ananto's voice rose above the shower running in the bathroom.

Jibon's face betrayed both a smile and regret. He had been dreaming of playing Test cricket since the age of twelve. He had scored eight centuries last year in local cricket matches, and eleven so far this year. But he hadn't even got a chance to play a first-class match for Bengal. How would the national selectors consider him if they couldn't watch him play?

There had been an hour of celebrations in the Friends' Society dressing room at the CAB clubhouse after the match. It was deserted now. Everyone had left for the club tent. The rest of the festivities—a feast, fireworks, garlanding of the players, promises of gifts, flag-hoisting—would continue there.

Only the club groundsman Mohon was still in the

room. He was busy putting the equipment into their long bags. The P. Sen Trophy would be starting in a few days. No one would take their personal things home today. Going up to the window, Jibon frowned.

'Seen the sky, Mohon-da?'

'Nor'wester.'

Black clouds had gathered over the river in the west. Three or four hawks were swooping about. The clouds were rushing eastwards. The past few days had been hot and sultry. Calcutta had prayed for rain constantly. On trams and buses, people kept repeating as often as they could that it had never been hotter. Finally there was a cold, wet whiff of rain. The breeze that had sprung up hit Jibon on his face as soon as he went out into the President's Enclosure.

'Ahhhh!' The sigh of relief popped out of his mouth unbidden. His throat had expelled the same sound earlier when he hit a six off the last ball to get a one-wicket win for his club. It was a signal of release from tension. He had got to his hundred in the previous over.

How hot must it be today? Shutting his eyes and placing his face in the stream of cold air, Jibon tried to make a guess. It had been 39° Celsius the previous day. 'Where's the sense in playing in these conditions?' his father had said. 'Who can give his best? It'll just damage your body. These matches still make sense before the knock-out stage of the Ranji Trophy—a good performance can get you a place in the team. But Bengal's already lost in the quarters, what's the point of these games now under this blazing sun? At least you've been saved by the semi-final defeat in the J.C. Mukherjee Trophy, you won't have to play the final.' Jibon had told his father softly, 'We have to avenge that seven-wicket loss to Agragami. The run-out decision against me—' he had stopped, remembering something Antu had said. Back in the pavilion after being adjudged run-out, Jibon had flung his bat across the room, screaming, 'Cheating, nothing but cheating! I had my bat down six inches behind the crease at least three seconds before the ball hit the stumps.' Putting his hands on Jibon's shoulders, Antu had said, 'Never complain after getting out. There's a god above. The umpire can always make a mistake. He's human, after all. The one up there corrects the mistake. We're playing them again in the knock-out final. If he understands your unhappiness he'll look after you. But don't complain again. You'll never make it to the Test-level if you complain.'

From the clubhouse, Jibon smiled at the field and the emptiness of the enormous stands. Then he looked up at the sky to offer his thanks to that person upstairs. The thick clouds were speeding towards him, darkness was closing in. The treetops were swaying madly. Birds were beating their wings desperately to stop themselves from being blown away. Jibon's heart trembled suddenly with an unknown fear. Was this how god showed himself? He adopted the pose of a praying man, almost unconsciously.

'Do you know how many times I've been calling you? What, now that you've won the match for us nothing but praise will do? Come on, enough congratulations for one day.'

'You believe in god, don't you, Antu?'

'Baba used to say, you must have faith in something. It will anchor you, won't let you be swept away. It could be faith in god, or in your motherland, or in the people of your country, or in friendship.'

'Which one's yours?'

'All of them.'

Fat drops of rain began to fall noisily. Their bare bodies were being drenched by gusts of wind and rain. His eyes glittering, Jibon suddenly held his arms out, screamed 'Yahooooo!' and raced towards the staircase. Kicking the iron door open, he ran onto the field, stopping on the grass. Raising his arms towards the sky, he turned to Ananto.

'Antu, I'm going to play in Tests,' Jibon shouted. 'Can you hear me, Antu, I'm going to play in Tests. God has sent word that I'll play.'

Antu couldn't hear anything over the sound of the

torrential rain. 'Don't get wet,' he shouted anxiously. 'You'll get pneumonia.'

Jibon's figure in the middle of Eden Gardens was blurred. He was rolling around on the field in ecstasy.

'What's the matter with Jibon? Is he going mad or something?'

Mohon was standing beside Ananto.

Shaking his head, Ananto said, 'Jibon will play in Tests one day, take my word for it, Mohon-da.'

'And you?'

Ananto smiled, shaking his head in a way that left the meaning unclear.

'Jibon's scooter is parked in the open. I'll go find a covered spot for it somewhere.'

About to turn towards the staircase, Ananto glanced at the ground again. Indistinctly through the rain he saw the five-foot-three Jibon—exactly a foot shorter than him—lying on the ground, facing the sky, his arms spread out. Like an inert dead body. For a moment, Ananto's heart leapt into his mouth.

They left for the club tent half an hour later, after the rain had stopped. The scooter was wet but the engine hadn't been affected. It was three minutes from the CAB clubhouse. Jibon took the turn around the roundabout in front of the All India Radio office very sharply, the scooter tilting. Seated behind him, Ananto clutched his shoulder. 'Don't take turns at such high speed, the road's slippery.'

Jibon neither answered him, nor lowered his speed. Ananto didn't say anything more. This was how Jibon was. It was evident in his batting too. He took great risks to play shots which made the purists raise their eyebrows. 'He won't get too far if he plays this way,' they said, shaking their heads in disapproval. 'He'll never make it to the Tests.' But Jibon scored heaps of runs, centuries too.

Even Ananto had told him once, 'Have you heard what they say about you? "No big match temperament".' Jibon had feigned astonishment. 'Have I even played a big match for people to have figured out my temperament? Is the batsman supposed to display his temperament or make runs? I take batting simply—the ball's there to be hit, so hit it. If you can't hit it, leave it or block it. The ones with temperament are excellent at the last two, but they're afraid of the first. So we lose matches we should be winning.'

'And save matches we would be losing.'

'I don't play with thoughts of losing or drawing a game.'

Today it was Jibon who had got them victory. Not only had he scored a century off 67 balls, he had also carried the innings from 51 for 7 to 172.

The celebrations had waned in the tent, but they began again when the two of them arrived. Ananto had taken 1 wicket for 31 runs, and got a run-out with a throw from mid-on. He got some perfunctory congratulations. He didn't mind. There was only one hero of the day. Cricket Secretary Badol Dey took the expensive watch off his wrist and fastened it around Jibon's.

'What's this, what's all this Badol-da, I have a watch. What'll I do with another?'

'Wear one on each hand. After Gavaskar scored two centuries in the same Test in Pakistan, the Indian manager Gaekwad gifted him his own watch. I'm giving you mine.'

Badol Dey looked around jubilantly, his jaws thrust out. Becoming the Cricket Secretary for the first time and winning a trophy immediately meant he was a lucky Secretary for the club. Everyone looked at him admiringly. One of them even said, 'Why will the boys play well without incentives? P. Sen trophy next. I'll give a gold ring to whoever brings us the trophy.'

There was a buzz of approval.

Jibon raised his arms. There was a watch on each wrist. 'Which one should I check the time on, Mr Gaekwad?'

'Ask Gavaskar,' Ananto quipped softly.

'No chance of meeting him. Gavaskar will have retired from first-class cricket by the time I make it to the Bengal team.'

'Who says that's far away? Next season, take it from me. Who else has nineteen centuries in two seasons?' Badol Dey's scream silenced everyone. Ananto stole out to the portico with a soft drink.

The sky was still overcast. There was moisture in the air. The evening would quietly slip in any moment. The leaves had turned a deep green with the rain having rinsed the dust off of them. Some of the streets were waterlogged. By now, his mother must be home from the college where she taught. She had stopped him when he was about to touch her feet out of respect this morning, before leaving. 'Him first.' A photograph of his father hung on the wall of the covered veranda, which they used as a combined drawing and dining room. A garland of stale marigolds hung around it. His third death anniversary had passed four days ago.

Ananto was thinking of the words he had muttered, his forehead touching the photograph. 'I remember everything you told me, Baba. I will work hard, and I will be patient.' Turning to his mother, he had found her gazing at his father's photograph, a beautiful smile radiating from her eyes. He had touched her feet then.

'Both the teams can't win, one of the two has to lose, Antu. I'm saying the same thing your father did: keep trying, never give up.'

Ananto had not given up today. Just effort wasn't enough, though, you needed some luck as well. Two catches had been dropped off his bowling. His pace had defeated the batsmen seven or eight times, just that the ball hadn't hit the stumps. Like all other fast bowlers, he too wanted to see the stumps flying in the air. Why couldn't he hit them? That was when he thought he heard his father's voice. *You haven't worked hard enough, Antu. A fast bowler has to break his back with effort. You're neglecting length and direction, and concentrating on pace alone. You're making a mistake.*

Ananto was startled by someone clapping him on his back.

'What are you staring like that at the sky for? Are you meditating or something?'

Jibon was still in the grips of ecstasy. He offered the box of sweets in his hand to Ananto, who took one.

'Everyone's saying Badol-da must take us out to dinner. Coming?'

'I don't like eating out.'

'Me neither. I never feel I've had a meal when I eat with a fork and spoon. Baba got a big hilsa fish this morning. Come to our place.'

'Ilish in May!'

'From Bangladesh, it's outstanding.'

Ananto's mouth watered at the thought of slices of ilish on his plate. Lowering his voice, he said, 'Get the scooter out, they'll stop us if they find out we're not going to the restaurant. We'll have to get away quickly.'

They made their escape.

~

Jibon's was an affluent family. His father owned a business for manufacturing electronics components. They had moved to a new house in Kankurgachi in Calcutta a year ago. Every member of this family of four was small in stature, none of them taller than five-foot-three. Ananto had felt rather awkward on the first day he met them. Jibon's father, Deben-babu, was a jovial man. Sensing Ananto's awkwardness, he had joked, 'Look who's here, Gulliver himself. Now you're in trouble visiting the Lilliputs at home, aren't you? Don't worry, I'll get a low stool for you to sit on and stilts for all of us.' Ananto had grown fond of them, visiting Jibon at home often in the past year and a half. They took special care of him because his father was dead, treating him like their own son.

As they were driving back, Ananto said, 'When you ran into the ground shouting "Yahoo," I was reminded of that first day, "Look who's here, Gulliver himself."'

Turning his head, Jibon said, 'Why?'

'Swift had called one of the imaginary races in *Gulliver's Travels* "yahoos,"' answered Ananto, leaning forward to speak into Jibon's ear.

'Do you read a lot?'

'Sometimes.'

'I don't like reading,' said Jibon, changing gears and accelerating.

'You like speed,' said Ananto.

Jibon just nodded.

'Don't drive fast today. The road's not in good shape, too many potholes.'

'I know it like the back of my hand. Every pothole, every bump.'

Jibon's room was in the northeast corner of the first floor. One wall was covered with posters of cricketers. It was the short batsmen who caught the eye in that array—Bradman, Gavaskar, Weekes, Vishwanath, Kallicharan. A messy room. Ananto had often stayed the night here.

Jibon asked him to stay back tonight as well. Ananto didn't want to. He had eaten his rice with six pieces of fried ilish and the oil in which the fish had been fried. His finger still smelt of the food, though he had soaped them twice. Sniffing his palm, Ananto said, 'I gorged so much today, Kakima, it'll take me a week to get back in shape. There's another tournament coming up.'

'If a thimbleful of rice is going to make you unfit, why bother with sports? I don't understand this bias against rice. Apparently it's the root of all un-fitness.'

Ananto chuckled. Earlier he used to have chapatis for dinner, but for the past six months he had switched to them for lunch too. Yet Jibon's mother was convinced that the tall and lithe young man was actually weak and sickly, just because he avoided rice. She would insist on ladling mountains of rice on his plate and Ananto would raise his arms, bleating piteously, 'I'll lose my fitness.' It was the same tonight. But Ananto added, 'So much better than eating at a restaurant, right Jibon?'

Strapping the watch that Badol-da had gifted him on his right wrist, Jibon said, 'It's not like Bengalis can dream of a better meal in the world than fish and rice.'

'It's so late, Ananto, why not stay back tonight?' Jibon's father said, attacking his mouth with a toothpick.

'Ma doesn't know, she'll worry.'

'Will you get a bus at this hour?'

'I'll take a train from Bidhan Nagar station to Dum Dum and walk the rest of the way.'

Glancing at his watch, Jibon said, 'Let me take you to the station.'

Wheeling his scooter out, he said, 'Feels like a condemned man's last meal, my stomach's hurting.'

'You'd better sit at the back then, let me drive.'

Jibon took the pillion seat without protesting. As soon as Ananto started the engine and released the clutch, the scooter shot off with a jerk. Ananto's hands began to shake. He stopped and switched the engine off.

'Not used to a scooter,' he said apologetically.

'How will you get used to it till you try, come on now. How many times have I told you to buy one?'

Ananto started the engine again and released the clutch gingerly. This time they started off smoothly.

'Ma doesn't want me to. She's terrified of two-wheelers. She thinks it's dangerous to drive them given the state of Calcutta's roads.'

'You'll never be a fast bowler if you're always afraid. I won't be able to face fast bowling either, if I am.'

Ananto concentrated on driving. The streets were still waterlogged. Half of the road they were on, from the pavement to the middle, was still submerged. Only the spine rose above the water. Ananto rode slowly down this central portion. The streetlights were dim, the shops were closed, and everything looked dark. The road was lit up occasionally by the headlights of passing cars, blinding Ananto. He swerved to the left, and a speeding car behind him began to blow its horn. Ananto moved even closer to the pavement.

'Faster, faster, why are you giving way?' Jibon asked impatiently. Ananto accelerated in response.

He had learnt to drive on this very same scooter of Jibon's. Whenever he had stayed over, Jibon had given him lessons on the deserted roads of the neighbourhood, here on the eastern fringe of Calcutta, early in the morning. It was full of apartment complexes, amusingly named after great men. Vivekananda,

Surendranath, Ishwarchandra, Bidhanchandra. The complexes built on a cooperative basis had names like Purbasha, Udichi, Ideal, Elite. The names revealed the tastes and mentalities of the residents. One of the roads was named Bidhan Shishu Sarani. Ananto had found it funny that a street was named for children. 'Maybe because children live here,' Jibon had said. Spotting a four-storied building named Skyline, he had said, 'If a building of my height is called Skyline, what will a twenty-storey one be called?' Ananto had said. 'Heavenline.'

An enormous truck was stalking them, blowing its ear-splitting air-horn.

'Don't give way, don't move,' Jibon instructed angrily from the back.

'The rules say you must make room for larger vehicles.'

'To hell with your rules. Is our scooter a toy?'

The truck was close enough now for a collision—barely two or three yards behind Jibon. The man next to the driver had his head out of the window, and was yelling.

The two truck headlights were bathing the occupants of the scooter in light.

The man beside the driver threw an expletive at them. 'Stop, Antu,' Jibon shouted. 'I'm going to drag that fellow out and give him a hiding. Antu, stop.'

'No.'

'Stop at once,' Jibon roared.

Reaching out from the back, he pulled at Ananta's right hand gripping the handle of the scooter. The vehicle tottered. The wheel turned to the left, and entered a pothole submerged in water. The scooter skidded to the right and fell on the road.

Ananto heard the harsh screech of the truck-driver slamming on the brakes. He had fallen on his back on the pavement in a puddle of water. He could see a tree with dense foliage, and a dark sky through the gaps. A void in his head. The sound of the truck receding in the distance.

Ananto sprang to his feet. A car was approaching from a distance. In the beam of its headlight he saw the scooter lying on the road like an upside-down cockroach. The engine was off, the rear wheel was rotating slowly to a stop, and Jibon was trying to prop himself up in a sitting position with his left arm. The left half of his body was under water.

The car was nearer now. The scene was clearly lit up.

'Jibon!' shrieked Ananto. Turning his face towards Ananto, Jibon said, 'You're too tall, Antu, bend towards me.'

Ananto bent towards him.

'I'll never play a Test Match, Antu.'

Jibon looked at his right arm. Ananta saw nothing

but flesh between the tips of the fingers and the wrist, the bones pulverized into a red sheet, and the dial of the watch still sitting in its place.

'No, Jibon, no. You WILL play in Tests. I'll make it happen.'

Ananto had no idea why the words came out as a heartrending scream.

2

Thirty months after this accident, a report by a staff reporter of the *Anandabazar Patrika* appeared on November 15:

> '*No, I don't want anything more. Just a Limca, please.' I was surprised to see the speaker pick up a glass of Thums-Up with a trembling hand. He wasn't drunk, but he was on the verge of losing his balance. The speaker's name: S. Panigrahi. The President of the Board of Control for Cricket in India.*
>
> *None of us had expected to see this dignified and grave gentleman in such a state. He was accompanied by L. Hariharan, the BCCI Secretary. Hariharan is a lawyer by profession and a formidable one from all accounts. He was in a similar state. Fifteen minutes of melodrama had preceded this scene at a press conference at Delhi's Taj Palace Hotel.*
>
> *It all began when, twenty-four hours before the first ball of the first Test in the five-match series against*

Australia was to be bowled, a member of the BCCI informed the journalists, who were watching the net practice at Feroz Shah Kotla, that a press conference had been scheduled at 3 PM that afternoon in Room No. 402. Please be present, he had requested the journalists.

Several journalists had stayed away, assuming it was a routine pre-Test press conference. Those who were absent were deprived of an extraordinary occurrence. On entering the room we found the President and Secretary of the Board sitting with their heads bowed, despondency and fatigue in their eyes.

'We have some news to give you,' began Panigrahi. 'Only four of the fourteen cricketers selected for the Test series have accepted all the conditions in the contracts we gave them. They are Arvind Nabar, Chand Gowda, Deshraj Anokha, and Mohammed Usmani. The other ten have signed the contracts but rejected three of the conditions. These are: not writing for newspapers and magazines without the permission of the Board, not using any other logos, and not playing in tournaments not sanctioned by the BCCI.'

Panigrahi read out the names: Madhurkar, Pillai, Pushkarna, Bhojani, Kapur, Farzand Ahmed, Gupta, Dharaddhar, Dua, and the captain Makarand Varde. Sounding broken, the Board Secretary added, 'They have betrayed us. Even this morning all of them had assured me that they would accept all the conditions and sign the contract. I hadn't expected to be let down at the last minute.'

The reason for their state of mind was obvious now. The first Test with Australia was to start the next day. The final eleven was to be selected an hour before the game. But now there was a crisis. 'What's your view? What should the Board do?' The President asked the journalists directly.

One of the journalists had grown agitated. Jumping to his feet, he said, 'Drop them. Leave the whole lot out. They're playing at home, they should be concentrating on putting in the best possible performance, instead they're busy chasing money.' The others supported him. But the Board officials still appeared hesitant. 'We too would like to take a strong step,' said Panigrahi. 'But have you considered the reaction? The entire country will oppose us. And it isn't even possible right now. The outcome will be disastrous.'

There were concerted attempts to convince the Board officials that the people of the country would support a strong stand against the cricketers on this issue. But they weren't willing to take a risk. Things came to a point where a veteran journalist from Delhi had to say, 'It's because the Board is so spineless that the cricketers can dare to flout discipline this way.'

Instead of being angered, Panigrahi promised, 'We may be giving in for now, but mark my words, we'll get the better of them before this series ends.' It is difficult to say how he will fulfil his promise, for all ten of those cricketers will rebel in the event of any action taken against any one of them. Several senior cricketers gathered in captain Varde's room yesterday to decide that the skipper must be allowed to write in the newspapers every day. If the opposition captain could use his pieces to apply pressure, why not the Indian captain? We have been informed that the 'rebels' will communicate their decision to the board through a letter. Kapur and Madhukar will draft the letter. A furious conflict between the Board and the cricketers appears imminent. Both sides are determined to see it through to the bitter end.

It is needless to add that such a predicament on the eve of a Test Match will not be beneficial to the mental equilibrium of the cricketers. But if the Indian team can win the first Test, or even ensure an honourable draw, public opinion will swing in its direction. The Board will be unable to take any action in that case. But if the team loses, the cricketers will be cornered. The Board will not hesitate to teach them a lesson in that case. What form can this punishment take? Can the entire team be suspended? Who will play for India? The answers will be available soon.

Jibon picked up the newspaper with his left hand. He had read the article twice already. Still he ran his eyes over it once more, stopping at the words 'But if the team loses...'

He picked up his writing pad, where he had been jotting down the scores while watching the match on television. Varde had won the toss and chosen to bat. At lunch, India were 58 for 7. The innings folded in the fourth over after lunch, at 80. Lawton had taken 5 for 24 off 53 deliveries, Bright had taken 3 for 20 off 66 deliveries, and Ambrose and Steele had shared the other two, for 17 and 13 runs apiece. There were six extras. Bhojani had top-scored with 20, followed by Gupta, not out at 12, and Varde on 10. Three batsmen had scored ducks—Farzand, Dua and Pillai. Madhurkar was not playing because of a strained back, with Arvind Nabar taking his place. He was bowled for 1 after facing 8 balls. Karnataka's Mohammed Usmani was playing his first ever Test. He had faced 25 deliveries to score 5 runs in 42 minutes.

Jibon turned the page over. Frowning over the scores, he made some calculations. Australia was at 118 for 8 at the end of the day's play, after three hours of batting over 44 overs. So India had struck back. Eighteen wickets in a single day. The TV commentators kept harping on about the pitch. Some said it was under-prepared, others, that the ball was swinging late, seaming, jumping chest-high in the cloudy, windy conditions. One of them even said that Indian batsmen had neither the technique nor the courage to play fast bowling.

But it had indeed been a bewildering day of cricket. Lawton and Bright were both genuinely fast. Both of them had played over 40 tests, with more than 200 wickets each. John Irwin, one of the finest all-rounders in the world, with nearly 3,000 runs and 328 wickets, was not even playing this Test. Even so, it was looking as though the match would be over in two-and-a-half days. Had 18 wickets ever fallen on the first day of a Test match played in India?

It had to be admitted that India's bowlers had fought back. Even a batsman like Bolan, with over 6,000 runs in Tests and 17 centuries, could make only 9. Rogers, the opener, and Bright were the not-out batsmen, on 44 and 12, respectively. Lawton had made 19. The other six hadn't even reached double figures. Dua and Kapur had bowled aggressively, Dua taking four of the eight wickets, and Kapur, three. There was one run-out.

Jibon began to feel restless. What if India won the Test? You never knew, you could never tell where cricket was concerned. If they won, the Board wouldn't have the chance to teach them a lesson. The entire country would be hero-worshipping the cricketers. Who would have the guts to take disciplinary action against them? On the contrary, the same journalists who had accused the Board of being spineless and allowing players to flout regulations would turn out in support of the cricketers, arguing there was no harm in allowing them to write in newspapers. And that the game of cricket wouldn't be defiled if they wore logos of their choice. Winning was what mattered.

But not to Jibon. Something that Panigrahi had said was stuck in his head since morning: 'Mark my words, we'll get the better of them before this series ends.' And what an angry journalist had said: 'Drop them. Leave the whole lot out.' As these two statements whirled around in his head, his emotions churned while watching the Indian batting line-up being demolished. He had been praying that India should lose, that India should be defeated. To teach these cricketers a lesson. To jolt them. Let all of them be dropped. Let there be a new team. In which case...

But Dua and Kapur had wiped out the 'in which case'. India had recovered. Would the two teams go neck and neck in the second innings too?

Jibon began to pace up and down. Going to the window, he gazed absently at the people and cars passing on the road. The pitch—there was no doubt that it was because of the pitch that eighteen wickets had fallen. How could technically sound batsmen like Varde or Bolan get out so easily? The dismissals were replayed in front of Jibon's eyes. The ball hit the deck, seamed in, rising waist-high. Both the batsmen were over six feet tall, they couldn't take their bat away in time.

But was the pitch going to stay this way? Wickets changed character, sometimes over the course of a day. If the pitch played truer tomorrow, would India be able to get to 250? Australia would have to play the fourth innings. What if the pitch deteriorated? If Dharaddhar and Pushkarna found their lines with their orthodox left-arm spin, and Farzand with his off-spin, and the ball turned significantly, in that case…

Picking up the pen with his left hand, Jibon began to sketch a face with wavering lines. In that case the same team would go on playing. Not more than two or three of the Australians could play quality spin bowling. Jibon suppressed a sigh. 'No hope of playing a Test,' he scrawled beneath the portrait.

The letters were misshapen, tilted, irregularly sized and spaced. Every day he practised writing with his left hand. It looked neat when he wrote slowly, but became messy when he scribbled. His arm had had to be amputated four inches above the wrist the day after the accident. He had a prosthetic in its place. To hide it he wore skin-coloured cotton gloves and loose, long-sleeved kurtas. He could now do some things with his right hand, such as holding a book when reading it, drawing the curtains, and even steering a car. He had flown kites too without any trouble.

Tossing the pad on a desk he went to his own room. The walls were unadorned, without a single poster. No cricket equipment either. He put on a sleeveless sweater, and then a kurta over it. Picking up the car keys and his wallet, Jibon went downstairs.

His father was out on work, his mother was visiting a friend, and he had no idea where his brother was. 'Are you planning to drive, Borda?' the servant asked.

'Yes, can you open the garage doors?'

His mother had protested against the idea of buying a car. Naturally. She was unwilling to let her son drive, no matter whether the vehicle had two wheels or four. But his father was ready. 'Jibon has not become a cripple, he is normal,' he had told his wife. 'A small part of his arm is missing, but everything else is fine. Why must you consider him helpless or unfit? It's more important to ensure he doesn't think of himself that way. If he considers himself handicapped he will be upset, he will not be able to establish himself. His mental equilibrium will be disturbed if he starts considering himself a burden on anyone. Is that what you want? Allow Jibon to forget he has lost a part of a limb. Let him think himself as a normal person, as normal as anyone else.'

'But he could have died,' said Jibon's mother. 'He was saved only by the grace of god.' His father had smiled. 'Any of us can die anywhere and anytime in an accident. Does that mean no one drives? I'm certain he can overcome his difficulties.'

Jibon's father had bought him this second-hand Premier a year-and-a-half ago. He had been driving smoothly and flawlessly ever since. Today too he negotiated his way through a logjam of minibuses.

Only at one spot on the road, near a tree with a thick trunk, did he take his foot off the accelerator to slow down. Then, gritting his teeth and clenching his jaws, he floored the accelerator with his right foot. The car charged ahead like a frenzied bull towards Dum Dum, where Ananto lived.

3

An elongated lake stretched out to the right of the railway track. Three bedrooms, a kitchen and a bathroom ringed a veranda on three sides. The western side was unblocked, but protected with a collapsible iron gate. The veranda extended into a portico with a sloping roof of red tiles. Two steps below lay a thirty-foot expanse of grass, with scattered flowering plants. It was here that the husband and wife sat in their deckchairs in the late afternoon and early evening. The lake lay to the west, followed by the railway tracks and the setting sun. They would gaze at the sight, conversing softly. Their only son would sit down near them when he got back from his games. After chatting with them for a while, he would wash up, have a snack, and start studying. Both his parents were college professors. They too would get down to their reading or marking of exam papers. A middle-aged woman took care of the household and the cooking. The lights would go out precisely at ten at night, and at five a.m. the boy would unlock the collapsible door to go running with his father.

The house was situated on a sixty-foot-long plot of land. It stood on one side, with a twenty-foot kitchen garden next to it. Here the family grew onions, chillies, lemons, spinach, gourd, pumpkin and similar vegetables. Tending to the garden was the couple's way of relaxing.

One day the boy asked his father for some money to buy a rubber ball. He wanted to play cricket with his friends. His father not only gave him the money, but also stopped on his way back from work to watch them play. He had played for both the football and cricket teams in his school and college. Watching the children play, it occurred to him that his son had the potential to be a sportsperson. His physical prowess and competitiveness was greater than those of his friends. He decided to encourage his son to become a cricketer.

The first time that he had been to Eden Gardens to watch a Test was during the second time the West Indies was touring India. He was stunned by the fast bowling of Roy Gilchrist and Wesley Hall. He had felt goose-pimples on his skin, his heart beating faster every time either of the two players ran up to bowl. He couldn't believe his eyes as he watched them explode on the field. It had filled him with a sense of wonder that he had never forgotten. Arun Sen decided that he would groom Ananto to be a pace bowler.

He began by buying books that taught the techniques of cricket. He knew nothing about fast bowling, but the books gave him some ideas. What he realized, however, was that the real learning would come not from reading books but by watching great bowlers in action. Every Sunday in winter, he would take his son to the Calcutta maidan to watch cricket games, their lunch packed in a bag. When the players broke for lunch, so did they. During the game he would explain the finer points of fast bowling to Ananto. Arun Sen replaced the kitchen garden with a cricket pitch where his son could practise. His wife Tonima had not complained. On the contrary, she had quietly supported her husband and son's dedication. Theirs was a peaceful, happy family.

The small single-storied building was as simple and shorn of excesses as its inhabitants. Attractive without being packed with expensive furniture. Both Arun and Tonima subscribed to the principle of 'small is beautiful'. They believed that steering their lives in the direction of comforts and luxuries would distract their minds and time with meaningless paraphernalia, robbing them of their freedom. They ensured focus, clarity and untainted hearts for themselves by not allowing their existences to be fenced by extravagance.

It was this mentality that had made Arun Sen quit a high-powered job in a large company overnight. His boss had pressured him to certify that Rs 15-lakhs-worth, perfectly good chemical equipment was malfunctioning. He had refused to be part of a plan to sell the equipment on the grounds that it had gone bad and pocket a kickback. He had been tempted with a higher salary, a larger flat, a bigger car, the best medical support and even an annual holiday with his family. He had thirty years to go before retiring, which meant that these benefits were his to enjoy during that entire period.

Like every other day, that day, too, he had returned home from the office only around nine in the evening. Antu had fallen asleep. Arun Sen never managed to spend any time with his son while he was awake. He could not tell him stories or play with him. What was it that he could offer Antu in return for the lack of his company? A few extra bundles of currency notes, perhaps. Was this the best thing a father could leave for his son? He had never felt money was the best legacy.

'If I quit my job, we won't have our affluence, this flat or this car,' Arun Sen had told his wife. 'Will that be a problem for you?' He had known what Tonima's answer would be. Still he had asked. Ananto was five at the time. 'I certainly don't want Antu to grow up on the strength of dirty money,' Tonima had replied. Within a week Arun Sen had bought this house in

Dum Dum and sent in his resignation. With first class Master's degrees in chemistry, both of them got jobs as college professors within a month.

~

At the age of eleven, Ananto found a wallet on the road, which he handed over to his father. It contained a hundred and thirteen rupees, along with the name and address of the owner.

'Isn't it enough to buy a bat?'

'Do you consider it honest or dishonest to take money from a wallet which belongs to someone else?'

'I hate playing with other people's bats.'

'Answer my question first.'

'It's dishonest, which you know very well, so why…'

'But what I want to know is whether you know it.' Softening his sharp tone, Arun Sen said, 'Keep your life simple and straightforward, Antu. There are as many wrong things we can do as right ones, and the two are completely different. Don't waste time on something that you know is wrong, it will bring you no joy.'

'What if it had been one lakh rupees instead of a hundred and thirteen?'

'Morals and ethics do not change with numbers. If I keep the money, I'll know I'm doing something wrong, and I will hate myself for it. One lakh rupees isn't essential to my life, what's essential is that I like myself.' Arun Sen had drawn his son closer. 'If you don't like yourself, there's nothing or nobody you can like.'

A couple of days later Arun Sen discovered Antu bowling at the wall of the house all by himself instead of playing with others.

'What's the matter?'

'They called me an idiot and many other names for handing over the wallet to you.'

'So you won't play with them?'

'No. Didn't you tell me doing the right thing makes one like oneself?'

'Do you like yourself?'

'Yes,' Antu had said, looking into this father's eyes. 'But nobody likes me.'

'I do. I think the world of you. I'm proud that you're my son.'

A wide smile spread across Antu's face. All he said was, 'I *am* your son.'

'Of course.'

They sat in silence, their arms around each other. Father and son, teacher and student.

~

Arun Sen took his son to a well-established cricket club. It wasn't nearby, which meant Ananto had to travel some distance every day. One of Arun Sen's students played for the club in the district league. Ananto had been chosen for the school team. His hat-trick in the trial match for picking the under-15 Bengal team for the Vijay Merchant Trophy had been mentioned in the English papers. He was good at studies too. But because of his academic and sporting prowess, because he was playing for the Bengal school team, because he had got a one-thousand-rupee scholarship from the cricket control board, and because he had been chosen for a month-long national camp in Bangalore, Antu began to be ostracized by his friends at school. Arun Sen was not surprised. Being the best inevitably meant being lonely. Only one person could be the number one, after all. 'You're that person in your school when it comes to sport,' he said, gripping Ananto's shoulders. 'Does it make you lonely? So be it. But you aren't alone at all. I know it'll feel that way right now, but there are many other lonely people in the world just like you. Somewhere, sometime, all the number ones will find one another.'

Arun Sen had wanted to tell his son a lot more, but a young mind would not be able to absorb so much. That night he began writing in a notebook, starting with the words 'BABA'S ADVICE FOR ANTU' in block letters. Whenever something occurred to him that Antu should know about, he would jot it down here. He would pass on the notebook to his son when the boy was old enough to understand its contents.

On the first day he wrote:

As you grow older you'll hear people mocking the noble qualities that enabled our enormous, ancient land to fight against the colonial rulers and wrest independence from them. These qualities are honesty, humility, hard work, determination, respect for elders and leaders, commitment, and patriotism.

It was your honesty that made you hand over the wallet to me, Antu. Your friends called you an idiot for this. They had wanted to spend the money. That would have been as good as theft. Stand firm, my son. If the fear of losing friends makes you sacrifice all that you have learnt, only so that you can count a group of thieves as your friends, you will not have gained much.

'You don't need a television right now,' Arun Sen said. 'I know you want one, and so do I. But I can only provide you with the things that you really need—food, shelter, education, and the kind of parents who are worthy of giving you their love and have the time for it.'

'Two of my classmates said their parents have bought TVs on monthly instalments. So can we.'

'Maybe we can. But first, tell me why a shop-owner is allowing you to pay in instalments. Because he's also charging interest for selling the TV to you on credit. Eventually you will end up paying three thousand rupees for something that costs two and a half thousand. Does it make sense to pay more for something because you cannot pay the entire price at once? I cannot afford a TV set right now, Antu, let there be no more discussions about this.'

That night Arun Sen wrote:

Antu, I want very much to buy you a TV set, but that will mean dipping into our savings. And it is those savings that give us peace of mind. Neither your mother nor I coach students privately, or else our income would have been much higher. We have to live within our means. We have chosen to do this so that we can spend more time with you, so that we have greater freedom on the path of courage and integrity, so that we can point you towards the positive aspects of life, so that you can be happy. This is how your mother and I think about it, and we believe it is working. A TV set would bring all of us some pleasure, but it would also mean changing our plans.

Life has a pattern, however. One thing leads to another. If our savings are depleted, I will have to consider private coaching, which will mean I will no longer be able to spend the evenings with you and your mother.

The quarter-final of the Vijay Merchant Trophy between East Zone and Central Zone was played at the CC & FC grounds in Calcutta. Ananto was staying with the team at a hotel on Free School Street. Tonima was ironing his clothes the night before he was to move to the hotel. Ananto was drinking a glass of milk, but it suddenly slipped out of his fingers. Arun Sen was reading a book. 'Nervous?' he said, lifting his eyes.

Ananto protested in embarrassment. 'It's natural to be nervous,' Tonima said. 'All these grown-up boys lying about their age to play in the junior team, and this little boy against them…'

'What if they are lying? Antu has to fight in order to win, isn't that right, Antu? Cricket isn't physical combat, after all. The young can beat the old with skill and intelligence. Winning is the main thing, there's no substitute for it.'

'You need some luck too, Baba.'

'Yes, that's true. But you know what, if you can get into the habit of being ahead of everyone, you will consider it your natural position and will do everything possible to stay there. But if your usual place turns out to be number four or five, the desire to do better dies. Which is what has happened to Bengal cricket.' Now Arun Sen felt he was putting too much pressure on this tender young man. So he added, 'But then not everyone can win all the time. And a defeat doesn't mean the end of the world either. The most important thing is to never give up. Win or lose, you must be able to tell yourself that you tried your best.'

Tonima was arranging the ironed clothes in a small suitcase. 'Ma's packing as though I'm going to play at Lord's,' Antu said. 'This is just an under-15 Vijay Merchant game, Ma.'

'You might be playing at Lord's one day.'

'My goodness! Lord's?' Antu's expression suggested he had swallowed something very sour. 'Talk about building castles in the air! The dreams can come later, let me win this trophy first.'

'Later? Why later? If you postpone your dream you'll postpone its realization too. Building castles in the air isn't foolish at all. Almost a hundred and forty years ago, a nature-loving American philosopher named Henry David Thoreau built himself a tiny wooden cabin, ten feet long and six feet wide, beside Walden Lake, two kilometres from his home. It had cost him a mere twenty-eight dollars. Then Thoreau wrote…' Tonima smiled at her husband. 'What's that line again?'

'If you have built castles in the air, your work need not be lost; that is where they should be. Now put the foundations under them.' Arun Sen smiled back at his wife. 'Did I pass the test?'

Central Zone scored 317 for 8 on the first day of the match. Batting at number three, Mohammed Usmani was 146 not out. Ananto had bowled 16 overs and given away 65 runs without taking a wicket. Arun Sen watched the game from the boundary lines. He felt the wicket was lifeless, offering no bounce. A strong wind was taking the swinging ball away from its line. Diving to his right in an attempt to take a return catch, Antu had injured his right shoulder. Besides, Usmani's technique for playing pace bowling was sound. He also felt that Antu was uncomfortable having his father among the spectators.

East Zone won the match by six wickets. Central Zone were all out at the same score, 317, on the second day. Ananto picked up both wickets within the first four balls of his first over. Usmani was yorked. Thanks to a belligerent innings of 171 by a young man named Jibon Guhathakurta, East Zone gained a first innings lead of 13 runs. Central Zone were all out for 147 in the second innings, with Ananto taking the first three wickets. East Zone reached their target for the loss of four wickets, Jibon playing another swashbuckling innings of 53.

In the semi-final East Zone lost the toss to West Zone. Put in to bat, they scored 294, with Jibon alone making 91. He was run out after a seventh wicket partnership of 53 runs with Ananto. Arun Sen went to watch the match, but kept himself out of sight of his son. He realized that the fault for the run-out was Ananto's. Lacking the muscles for a sprint, Ananto had hesitated over the second run and sent Jibon back. Jibon couldn't make it to the crease in time. But the run had been there for the taking. Arun Sen was disappointed that Jibon couldn't get two successive centuries.

The match ended when West Zone were 211 for 8. The outcome was decided with a toss. Ananto took 6 for 60.

Two days after returning home, Ananto discovered to his surprise that his father had bought weights, pulleys and ropes, and set them up. Also a heavy canvas bag of the kind which students used to carry their schoolbooks.

'Jibon Guhathakurta didn't get his century because your body wasn't strong enough for the boots, pads and bat. Running between the wickets is very important. You must run longer distances starting tomorrow, and within six months you must be able to run at least five kilometres effortlessly. You must fill this bag with iron weights, then do push-ups with it on your back and sit-ups with it on your shoulders. Your diet has to change too. Here, I've brought soyabean. Fish and meat are not as important. Your low-fat, high-nutrition diet will be built around dal, vegetables, fruit and milk. All of us are going to have to eat our chapatis with bran added to the flour. Doesn't matter if we don't like it, we'll get used to it in a day or two. Chocolate, ice-cream, sweets—you mustn't touch anything with sugar in it. We cannot eat like a Bengali family, or your body will never be strong enough.'

Arun Sen continued sharply after a pause, 'You must be expecting some praise for your six wickets.'

One look at his father's face and Ananto knew that merciless criticism was on its way. 'Never mind six wickets, even ten wickets in such matches have no value,' he said to shield himself.

'What do you mean! You've played an entire match to earn your wickets, you've been able to use your experience—are you saying these things have no value? You didn't get as many wickets on the same pitch in the last match. Why not? There will be many unexpected factors in your games from now on—featherbed wickets, dropped catches, bad conditions, injuries, and much more—all of which will prevent you from bowling with your natural rhythm. That's why you have to become a better bowler, much much better, so that you can overcome all such obstacles, so that you can even bowl with a broken foot. That's what you must prepare yourself for.'

'If I work very hard do you think I can bowl like Dennis Lillee or Andy Roberts, Baba?'

'Why not! You have the talent, and you're willing

to work hard. That's two of the three requirements for success. The third is the hunger to succeed. When you desire something as rare as success, you have to outrun the rest of the world to grab it. You have to desire it so intensely that no effort will seem too much, no amount of pain will seem sufficient, no loneliness will appear unbearable.'

That same evening, Ananto put down stumps in the kitchen garden, strung up a net behind them, and began to bowl. He added a table-lamp because the light outside the building was not strong enough. He had to start his run-up from across the road. A page torn out of a notebook was pinned to the ground at the good-length spot, one foot outside the off-stump. He had only two old cricket balls. His task was to pitch the ball on the white sheet of paper and make it cut back to hit the leg stump.

Two people were passing on the street outside in the near-darkness. They stopped abruptly.

'Look! Can you see what's going on?'

'What do you want me to see? It's just a boy practising his bowling.'

'No, near the net, must be his mother, see how she's bowling the ball back to him.'

The Cricket Control Board held a one-month coaching camp for under-15 cricketers in Bangalore that year. Twenty-one players were selected from all over India, with Ananto being the only one from Bengal.

By train to Madras, and then, after a change of trains, to Bangalore. He would have to spend two nights in trains. On the morning of his departure, Arun Sen handed a hundred rupees to his son, saying, 'Don't buy any food on the train. What your mother has given you will last you till Bangalore. Buy some dry food on the way back. You should have some money left over even after paying for taxis and rickshaws. Remember this isn't a pleasure trip. There's a great deal you don't know, a great deal you must still learn. You now have a chance to acquire that knowledge. Use it. You have to push yourself. Your parents won't guide you forever. A time will come when you will be in charge. Playing cricket is like walking a tightrope suspended between two mountain peaks. Failure means falling. And falling means death. So you simply have to be the best if you want to play Test cricket.'

'You'll write, won't you, Antu?'

Ananto only smiled at his mother. He wrote four letters in all from Bangalore. In the last one he wrote to his father:

I'll be able to demonstrate next season how I've benefitted from this camp. I've corrected a few errors, especially one on the follow through. Everyone's surprised to see I can make the old ball swing. They didn't believe me when I told them I practise in the garden at night. We saw the actions of the great fast bowlers on video. Lillee, Thompson, Holding, Roberts, Hadlee, Kapil, Willis. Also clips of Truman and Lindwall bowling.

We split into two teams and played two matches. I took three wickets in one game, five in the other. Usmani was in the other team for both games. I got him out to off-cutters both times, caught in the slips once and LBW the next time. He's furious with me, he looks away whenever we run into each other. What can I do? Apparently he's threatened to hit me out of the ground the next time we play on opposite sides. Usmani is a really good batsman. Stylish too. He'd have been in the Madhya Pradesh Ranji team if it hadn't been for a finger injury. He's bound to get into the Test team.

There's another pace bowler I liked. Deshraj Anokha from Punjab. His out-swing is even better than mine, and he bowls as fast as I do. He's a natural batsman too—he can hit sixes at will. I think it's him I'll have to compete with for a place in the Test team. So I'll have to concentrate more on my batting. I didn't get a chance to bat in the first game, and I made 23 not out in the second. I couldn't prove that I can bat better than most. But there's one more *match coming up, against the Karnataka veterans. This is where Anokha has an advantage over me. He's quick-tempered but not complicated. Our beds are next to each other. One night he said in the course of our conversation that he considers every batsman his enemy. So he never makes friends with a batsman outside the field. He doesn't want to develop a soft spot for them. Isn't that strange? He nurtures his hate for batsmen constantly. His argument is that this gives him extra power when bowling, he never loses energy. 'You should hate batsmen too,' he advised me. 'Don't you see how Usmani hates you. He's definitely going to take revenge.' 'You're my rival,' I told Anokha. He burst into laughter. 'I don't think of you as my rival at all, Ananto,' he said. 'A team needs two fast bowlers to open the bowling. If it's the West Indies, they need four. As for us, never mind four, we have just one medium pace bowler of Test class, Dua. In four or five years I will open the bowling for India from one end and you from the other.' I got goose pimples. What confidence!*

You get pure sandalwood here, powdered sandalwood too. The shops have lovely sandalwood figures. I'll take one for you, and powdered sandalwood and incense for Ma.

As Ananto was buying sandalwood from Cauvery on M.G. Road the day before leaving for Calcutta, nearly 1,500 kilometres away, Arun Sen suddenly felt a sharp pain in his head while teaching a class. Losing consciousness, he fell from his chair. A doctor came, and he was taken to a hospital nearby. He never regained consciousness. Tonima Sen was holding his hand when he died that evening.

4

Stopping in front of the house, Jibon blew the horn once to announce his arrival.

Ananto was exercising with the pulleys fixed on the wall of the portico. Sweat was streaming down his neck and shoulders, although it was November. The muscles on his back were glistening with perspiration. He didn't stop exercising at the sound of the horn.

Waiting on the steps for a minute or so, Jibon said, 'Did you watch the game today?'

'The first hour. Then we had a power-cut.'

'Know the score?'

Letting go of the pulley, Ananto rubbed his palms together. 'The electricity didn't come back till forty minutes after tea. I don't know what happened in between, but I know the score. It'll be a fantastic match.'

Ananto had been to Siliguri to play the final of a cricket tournament for a local club last season. The only condition he had set was that he should get a black-

and-white TV set. He took 8 wickets for 11 runs. The other two were run out. The TV set was placed next to the dining table. It was switched on only for the news and special programmes—neither mother nor son had a taste for light and mediocre things.

'It's not just the match, something fantastic might happen outside the field too. Did you read this morning's *Anandabazar*?'

'I did.'

'Don't you think the Board and the players are heading for a confrontation? There's bound to be a showdown.'

'What Panigrahi and Harihaaran said suggests as much. If they're talking of teaching the cricketers a lesson before the series ends, the Board must mean business.'

'What can they do?' Taking a clove from his left pocket, Jibon popped it into his mouth. 'You think the Board will dare touch them after today's performance?'

'Four days still to go.' Ananto held out his hand. 'Give me one.'

'The match won't run to five days on this wicket. Third day, at most till lunch on the fourth, no further.'

'Who'll win?' Chewing on the clove, Ananto got to his feet and jumped down the steps from the portico, saying, 'Where do you think you're going, Fulu?' A white cat was strolling on top of the wall. Grabbing it,

Ananto came back and sat on a chair. Putting the cat on his lap and scratching its neck, he said, 'It's difficult to say who'll win.'

'I want India to lose.'

'What! Of course not, I want them to win.'

'The Board can't take any action if they don't lose.'

'So the country has to lose just to make that possible?'

'Losing one more Test hardly matters. We've lost dozens already, what's one more? But the benefit is that this business of players breaking rules and ganging up against the Board will stop. If it isn't nipped in the bud right now, future generations will be affected too.'

'Is the players' demand unfair?'

'The money, you mean?'

'Yes. The Board has added crores to its fund, exploiting the players. Making them play non-stop, three series a year, countless ODIs. They've worked like dogs to make money for the Board. How many years did cricketers play earlier, Jibon, how many Tests in all?'

'Longer than players do now, but far fewer Tests.'

'Let's not even talk of Bradman, just fifty-two Tests in twenty years! Do you know how long Hammond or Woolley or Hobbes played first class cricket? Almost thirty years, each of them. Hammond played eighty-five Tests in that time, Woolley played sixty-four,

Hobbes played sixty-one. And how many have our Merchant or Mushtaq or Mankad or Hazare played? Pankaj Roy played forty-two in just ten years, Dattu Phadkar played thirty-one in ten, Mankad forty-four in just twelve…'

'Enough, take the pin off the record. I accept that today's superstars have burnt themselves out playing seventy or eighty tests and over a hundred ODIs in just ten years, but what does that have to do with breaking rules and being arrogant? Yes, they're playing more, but they're also getting paid more. That article says the players will revolt, that they're writing to the Board to insist that Varde be allowed to write in the papers, or else…'

'Blackmail?'

'What else?'

Ananto let the cat jump to the floor. Released, it stretched, puffed up its tail, and sauntered off.

'Why shouldn't there be protests against the Board's tyranny?' Ananto was worked up now. 'Does the Board dare to sack them?'

'Maybe they're waiting for the right time, and perhaps that time is now,' Jibon leaned forward. Lowering his voice, he said, 'In which case you might get to play, Antu.'

'What? How can I get to play?'

'If seven or eight of them are dropped, you're among

the ones in line to replace them. Usmani and Nabar have signed, they'll stay. Usmani has found a godfather in Hariharan after leaving Madhya Pradesh for Karnataka. Anokha and you will take Dua and Kapur's places. Your performance in the Duleep Trophy and Irani Trophy has been pretty good. You got thirty-eight wickets in the Ranji Trophy last season. The way the Indian bowlers hit back today, I felt you don't stand a chance, Antu. But on the way here it occurred to me that there's still hope if India loses. That's why I want India to lose.'

'So you *are* at home,' someone shouted from the road.

'Sachin-da, you?' Ananto walked up to the gate.

'The last time I came was two years ago. Ah, Jibon's here too.' Bald, dark and tall, Sachin-da took a chair in the veranda.

'No nets today?'

'I wanted to watch the game. Not going tomorrow either. Must watch the match.'

'What a match it has turned into already! Eighteen wickets on the first day! Ask for some tea.'

Ananto disappeared inside the house. Jibon spotted Tonima approaching from a distance. A white handloom sari with a black border, clasping a leather bag to her breast. Glasses with black frames. Ananto was built in the mould of her slim, tall, and proportionate figure.

'It's been so long, Sachin-da.'

'Yes, I don't think I've seen you at the Maidan since the accident. Three years, isn't it?' Sachin-da glanced at Jibon's right arm sadly. 'Fate,' he muttered.

Ananto came back. Jibon jumped in to prevent the conversation veering round to 'fate'. 'Watched the match today, Sachin-da?'

'How could I, we don't have a TV in the office.'

'Do you think the pitch was under-prepared or completely unprepared?'

'Who knows what they've been up to. Antu, let me tell you why I'm here. Narayan-da has asked you to meet him at CAB tomorrow, it's very urgent. He sent someone to the tent in the afternoon so that we could let you know.'

'What's the matter?' Like Ananto, Jibon also stared in surprise at Sachin-da. Narayan Sarkar was the Secretary of the CAB. A dignified man not given to doing anything without a reason or making meaningless small talk.

Tonima came in. Jibon stood up.

'How's your mother, Jibon?'

'She's well. She was asking when you're visiting us.'

'One of these days. There's not as much time as before.' Tonima went into one of the rooms. They had been in financial trouble after her husband's death, which was why she had had to start offering private coaching to students. She coached two young women at home twice a week, and ran a class with five others right here in the veranda, five times a week. In the morning she helped Ananto with his studies. He was due to take this B.Sc. final exam next year.

'Antu.'

A middle-aged woman called Ananto softly from one of the rooms. Ananto went in, returning with cups of tea and chanachur on a tray.

'Why do you think Narayan-da's sent for me?' Ananto looked at both of them.

Dropping Sachin-da at Shyambazar, Jibon looked up Narayan Sarkar in the telephone directory as soon as he got home and rang him.

'Hariharan rang me from Delhi this morning. He said Ananto must go to Hyderabad. The Australians are playing an under-25 India team there three days after the first Test. Ananto has to reach Hyderabad on the last day of the Delhi test. I've got his plane ticket, he should collect it tomorrow.'

'Why the sudden emergency call? They'd announced the team a week ago, Antu wasn't in it. Only the chairman of the selection committee can make a change, does the Board Secretary have the power to do it?'

'Pointless questions. The selection committee can even ask me to play if the Board wants it. There must be a reason for asking Ananto to go. I got the impression the Board is about to do something drastic. Hariharan kept saying this under-25 match will be very crucial for us as well as for some of the young stars. If they can come out with flying colours…he didn't say more.'

'You think they'll sack the entire team.'

The moments of silence that followed made Jibon's heart jump to his mouth.

'Probably.'

5

The Indian captain Varde's views on the first day's play were syndicated in several Indian newspapers via International Features. It began with an expression of surprise at the treacherous nature of the pitch, followed by an admission of helpless but mild criticism of fellow batsmen, and praise for Lawton and Bright, gratitude to Dua and Kapur for bringing India back into the match, a reminder that India would have to bat with great concentration and courage on the second day, and concluded with the hope that the pitch would crumble during the fourth innings, when Australia would struggle against world-class left-arm spinners like Dharaddhar and Pushkarna, and a classic off-spinner like Farzand. India's task now was to contain Australia within 150, and set a target of at least 225. The spinners would be able to bowl the Australians out on this wicket under 200 in the fourth innings.

Jibon knew that Varde was not the simpleton that

his piece made him sound like. Having played more than eighty Tests, he knew only too well that taking a lead of 225 on this wicket would be extremely difficult. But what he had written made it seem easy enough, so long as the batsmen applied themselves.

But Jibon wondered why it was necessary for the Indian captain to write such a piece. It was like a pedestrian match report. He found no support for the argument that if foreign captains could pressure their opponents through their columns, Indian captains should be free to do it too. Jibon had no idea whether Bolan had written a column, but he and everyone else in the country now knew that Varde had thrown a challenge to the Board—let's see if you dare to take action against us.

Another item of news caught his eye. Varde's second book would be formally launched on the rest day. Apparently it contained some bitter comments about a few of his fellow-cricketers, as well as the Board.

Today, too, Jibon planted himself in front of the TV set with his writing pad and pen. He was not anxious about Lawton or Bright, because he wanted India's second innings to fold below 150. Let the entire country be disappointed and annoyed with Varde's team. Let the Board sack them. That would mean a chance for Antu to play. The equation was simple. But first he would have to pass the test of the Hyderabad match. That would be the most important trial of his life.

Australia's innings ended at 128. Rogers remained not out with 48. India were trailing by 54 runs. Dua took the last two wickets, ending with figures of 6 for 55 off 14.1 overs. The Indian team applauded him as he led them out of the ground.

Pillai (5) and Usmani (0) were back in the pavilion with the total at 6. Both were bowled off yorkers in Lawton's third over. Nabar and Varde prevented any further fall of wickets till lunch, taking the score to 66 for 2. The funniest thing was that the pitch was playing absolutely normally. As sleepy and dead as the classic Feroz Shah Kotla wicket. No one would believe that just twenty-four hours ago India were 58 for 7 on the same wicket at lunch.

'Cricket!' muttered Jibon. 'You can never tell. They could still be all out for 70.'

After lunch Nabar got a boundary from a straight drive off Lawton, and was caught at gully off the very next ball. He had made 40 off 76 balls. Varde was on 18. Three overs later Pushkarna was poached at slip off Bright. 82/4, Varde on 26. He was settling down slowly, never playing in a hurry. Both the wicket and the bowling had lost their sting. Varde had scented a big score, and besides, he was on the verge of achieving the honour of scoring 5,000 Test runs. It would need an exceptionally good delivery to get him out now.

Despatching Ambrose to the ropes with an off-drive, Varde reached 39, earning the applause of the spectators for reaching 5,000 runs. A single off the next ball brought Bhojani to face Ambrose. The expert in the commentary box had stopped describing the action to list Varde's batting skills. Suddenly he exclaimed, 'Bhojani's been hit on the face!'

The fielders had rushed up to Bhojani, who was lying on the ground. Everyone was gathered around him. Some of them waved for a doctor, who ran in with two others. Bhojani was helped out of the ground, a handkerchief pressed to his face. He was on 10, and India, on 105. It wasn't clear whether he would be able to bat anymore. Kapur replaced him, with tea coming two overs later.

Kapur stormed to 44 before getting caught out leg before the wicket. Varde was on 61. India was 130 runs ahead. The way Gupta was playing, the bowlers made it clear that unless the wicket woke up, Australia would have no problem batting in the fourth innings. India were 210/5 at the end of the second day's play with Varde on 74 off 200 balls, and Gupta on 18. A lead of 162. The commentator announced that Bhojani had had seven stitches beneath his left eye, but hadn't suffered a fracture. He would bat if required.

India's second innings ended at 328 an hour after lunch on the third day. Australia had two and a half days to score 281 for a victory. They could win, but they could lose too.

Varde had got his century. On 102, he pulled a short-pitched ball from Ambrose into mid-wicket's hands. The camera had caught his face in a close-up as he walked back to the pavilion. He looked worried. He had mistimed his pull because the wicket had become even more placid. The ball had come slower than expected, and not risen either. The question on Varde's face seemed to be: can the spinners prevent 281 from being scored?

They couldn't.

But before that, the newspapers focussed on some of the paragraphs in Varde's book. He had written: 'The Board officials spend most of their time and energy in finding new ways to subjugate and browbeat cricketers. Apparently the honour and prestige of cricket are being marred by players writing columns and wearing company logos. The real reason for the heartburn is that if a cricketer dons a logo of a particular company, other sponsors lose interest. This causes losses to the Board and to the local organizers. The television authorities apply pressure as well. Why don't our Board officials take a look at tennis? Considering how many of the participants at Wimbledon wear their personal sponsors' logos, it wouldn't be an exaggeration to term the whole thing an industry. It is not acceptable that there can be one rule for cricket and a different one for tennis. Besides, when county cricket players in England can wear logos freely, why should it not be allowed for Test cricket? Even this simple argument will not be acknowledged by the impenetrable but twisted minds of the Board officials. Cricket administrators are suffering no personal losses in the process. Then why is this injustice being forced on cricketers?'

Referring to his being dropped from the Test team four years ago, Varde had written: 'The people who have learned discussions around a table to select the national team are nothing but a bunch of clowns. They'd be better off making circus audiences laugh.'

Elsewhere, he had commented: 'Many senior players in the team worry more about their own interests than about the match. Kapur and Pillai seldom attended team meetings. They were unwilling to cooperate with me on the field. On the fifth day of the Headingley Test during the last tour of England, when we had to score 57 runs for a victory with 6 wickets in hand, with Pillai and Kapur at the top of the bowling, both of them threw their wickets away to incredibly atrocious strokes. We lost the third Test by 16 runs. I am certain that had the two of them not committed suicide, the subsequent batsmen would not have been lost their heads. In fact, India would have won by 6 wickets."

It was during the same series in England that Varde had got into an argument on the field with umpire Stephen Rife at the Oval, on the fourth day of the fourth Test. When Rife turned down an appeal for a bat-and-pad catch against Robertson, Varde had told the bowler, Dharaddhar, from silly mid-on, 'Brilliant umpiring! That finger would have been pointing at the sky had the batsman been Indian.' Dharaddhar had said, 'The bastards won't be given out unless they're bowled.' Rife had heard the exchange. He retaliated with, 'You bloody Indians are cheats.'

Varde had written: 'It was impossible to keep one's cool after this. As Indians, being accused of cheating was beyond my wildest imagination. I gave him a piece of my mind as well. And then the storm broke. The next day Rife said, "I will not enter the field without a written apology." I said, "I'm willing to apologize if Rife is." But the TCCB took their own umpire's side. The fifth day's play did not start. Meanwhile the Indian team manager rang the Board President. In Delhi, South Block made enquiries with the Indian High Commissioner, who summoned our manager. I sensed trouble. The manager returned red-faced. "Play must be resumed at any cost," he declared. "Strict instructions from the foreign ministry in Delhi." Eventually, it was the Indian captain who had to pay the price by apologizing unreservedly. I handed the letter over to Rife the next morning forty minutes before the start of play. I was forced to do this. It shattered me. I had sought the support of the Board with all my heart, but it was not forthcoming. I had considered not playing at all and resigning, but I knew that if I didn't play, no one else would. All the players insisted on standing by me. They also gave a joint statement in my support. So I did not resign. The moral victory would have been Rife's if we hadn't played. The game was resumed and ended in an annoying draw. I had expected the Board to take action. It didn't. I had to swallow the humiliation.'

Quoting these excerpts from the book, the staff reporter of *Anandabazar* had commented:

Such an account from an Indian cricketer is not only unprecedented but also flouts the terms of the contract. This is not allowed according to the contracts between the players and the Board. And while Varde has written about having to swallow the humiliation, he has not mentioned the sweetener that came along with it. Two days after the incident, the President and Treasurer of the Board flew to London for a meeting with the team. They promised an additional five thousand rupees to each of the players, and fifteen thousand to Varde, to revive their flagging spirits.

Some of the players refused, saying, 'This is nothing but a bribe. We want our honour back, we don't want money.' But they had to give in to the majority. Varde swallowed his fifteen thousand rupees too.

Varde's book has exploded here like a bomb. There are rumours everywhere, with no one willing to speak up. All lips are sealed. Everyone I have asked has said they haven't read it yet. It is clear from their expressions that they have read the book, some of them more than once.

There are hints that three or four top Board officials will be holding a meeting today or tomorrow. They will hand Varde a show-cause notice over his newspaper column as soon as the match ends. At the same time the players will be asked to sign fresh contracts, with all the original clauses reinstated. If they refuse, the Board will not hesitate to take an extreme step. A showdown seems inevitable.

At the end of the third day Australia had made 80, losing both their openers. The nightwatchman, Goldie, ended his 40-minute innings at 1 in the sixth over of the morning. Australia was on 91 for 3, with all the wickets going to Farzand. But Goldie, who had 11 Test ducks, had played 38 deliveries. The way the batsmen were playing Farzand did not signal an imminent collapse.

Coming in to bat, Bolan made his intentions clear,

which was to go back with his team to the hotel an hour after lunch. Bright came in to replace Minter, who was caught at cover off Kapur for 31. Bolan was on 14, and Australia on 114 for 4. Lunch came 20 overs later, with Bolan on 52 and Bright on 44. Australia was 85 runs away from victory. In the fourth over after lunch, Farzand claimed his fourth scalp in the form of Bright. Australia was 203 for 5. An hour later, Bolan returned to the dressing room with Woodford, not out on 108 and 13, respectively. Having reduced Farzand and Pushkarna to schoolboy bowlers, when Bolan raised his arms to the sky after scoring his century in three hours, Jibon scribbled in his notepad, even happier than Bolan: 'The match is gone. You're probably playing.'

Australia won by five wickets, with a day and a half to spare.

Ananto rang in the evening. Answering the phone, Jibon said, 'Got the ticket?'

'Yes, the flight is in the afternoon tomorrow.'

'I'll pick you up at home and take you to the airport. Read the papers?'

'Varde's book?'

'Yes,' Jibon paused. 'Something unprecedented in India's cricket history is about to happen.'

'You think the Board will have the courage to do it?'

'They will. The result will give them courage. But

I think the conflict will continue till the Bangalore and Bombay Tests. You know why? India will lose two more Tests to Australia. Yes, they will. The one thing that TV coverage does is to give you a close-up of the players' expressions. Did you see their faces?'

'I did. They looked like they didn't want to play.'

'Because all of them are troubled. There's no such thing as team spirit anymore. They're looking like mercenaries. They won't be able to win a single Test in this series. All that's needed now is for public opinion to go against them. I rang Narayan Sarkar. Hariharan has told him the Hyderabad match is crucial for the Board. Which means they're looking for replacements. Now that they've called you, I have no doubt that that is the case. Antu, you can disappoint anyone you want, but not your father. He gave his heart and soul to preparing you for cricket. You have to ensure he finds his peace.'

Jibon's monologue ended. There was no response. Only after he had said 'hello' three times did Ananto say 'mmm?' as though he had just woken up from deep sleep.

'Your flight is at a quarter to three. I'll be there between one and one-fifteen.'

Ananto and Jibon reached the airport at two. 'I hate flying,' Ananto said on the way.

'Why? Do you know how much time you're saving?

A twenty-four-hour journey by train takes just two hours in the air.'

'I know, but I'm afraid.'

'Afraid?' This was the first time Jibon had heard Antu utter this word.

'I have a funny feeling in the pit of my stomach, and a cold hand seems to be clutching my heart. I keep thinking, what if the plane crashes?'

'Ohhh Antu, this doesn't suit you. Are you the only one on the plane? There are a hundred others with you, old people and babies…' Jibon slapped Ananto's thigh with his left hand.

Ananto stole a glance at Jibon's left arm. Three or four thick veins beneath skin, blood coursing through them. Faintly pink nails, elegantly tapered fingers, a broad wrist. And the other hand, the one on the steering wheel, had fingers and a wrist too, but… His heart almost stopped. 'All my fault, all my fault,' he told himself.

~

Soon after Ananto had queued up to collect his boarding pass and luggage ticket, passengers were told to go towards the security gates. Just one entrance each for men and women. The lines were already long.

'Look, Antu, that one's so much younger than you.'

A child of four or five was standing in the queue. Jibon gave Ananto a scathing look. He had found an excuse to tease his friend.

'He isn't old enough to know what fear is,' Ananto said.

'And you are, I suppose.'

Ananto looked away without answering. The queue was advancing slowly. Jibon walked with him as far as the security gate. As he was about to enter, Jibon said, 'I have to tell you something, Antu.'

'What?'

'You're too tall, Antu, bend towards me.'

Ananta's heart began to thud. The headlights of the car…the scooter upturned like a cockroach on the road…Jibon trying to raise himself on his left arm. 'You're too tall, Antu, bend towards me.' Ananto bent down. And then those words. 'I'll never play a Test Match, Antu.' What was it he had told Jibon then?

'No, I won't bend towards you. Tell me.'

'My heart says you'll make it to the Test team,' Jibon said, almost as though he was talking to himself.

'Keep moving there, why has the queue stopped?' someone said impatiently from the back. Ananto went in. He didn't look back. If he had, he would have seen Jibon waving at him with his left hand, his right hand hidden behind his back.

6

The under-25 team would have lost had Usmani not displayed extraordinary grit after the follow-on. Four senior players in the Australian team had gone to Agra to see the Taj Mahal, spent three days in Delhi on their way back, and travelled directly to Kanpur to play the second Test. They had not taken the Hyderabad game seriously.

After checking in at the hotel, Ananto asked the receptionist who his roommate was. He was relieved to hear it was Deshraj Anokha. The key to the room wasn't hanging on the board, which meant Anokha was in the room.

'Arre yaar, tum aa gaye.'

Anokha jumped to his feet when Ananto entered. 'It's been so long, nearly a year.'

'Ten months.'

They had last met during the Ranji quarter-final in Chandigarh in January. Ananto got 7 wickets in the match, but Punjab won on account of a first innings lead. Anokha took 11 wickets.

'Tea?'

'Yes.' Putting his suitcase on the wooden table in the corner, Ananto asked, 'Practice tomorrow morning?'

'At ten.'

After two-and-a-half hours of practice, the captain, Usmani, announced there would be a second session at four. Ananto and Usmani had met here for the first time at the dinner table. Usmani had said nothing more than a 'hello.' During the morning net practice at Lal Bahadur Stadium, when the batting began with the new ball after physical training, Usmani suddenly told Ananto, 'You can bowl later, let the regular bowlers start.'

Ananto was surprised. 'Am I supposed to be an irregular bowler?'

'Let those who are likely to be in the playing eleven get a chance with the new ball first. That's how I want it.'

'What's the problem if someone else bowls as well?'

'I want the batsmen to practise against the kind of new ball attack that Australia has. Your bowling is different, your turn will come later.'

Ananto found this reasoning rather strange. Four national selectors were present, including the chairman, which was unusual. Apparently, the Secretary and

President of the Board would be present too. The atmosphere was one of a Test match.

Usmani was the first to bat at the nets. Four bowlers began with the new ball. Ananto stood behind the net. He was burning with rage. One of the selectors, Central Zone's Mridul Sharma, asked him, 'How come you aren't bowling?' Ananto told him what Usmani had said. He nodded in appreciation. 'Intelligent chap. See how far ahead he thinks, how closely he's observed the Australian attack? He'll captain India one day, take it from me.'

As Usmani headed out of the nets towards a chair, he locked eyes with Ananto. 'May I bowl now?' Ananto asked, gritting his teeth.

'If you like,' answered Usmani disinterestedly.

Ananto bowled for half an hour at a stretch. His off-cutters were jumping from the good length spot. After one batsman was hit on the chest and another on the helmet, the team manager Anil Patwardhan told him, 'They're playing the match, Sen, getting injured won't help the team. Give them overpitched deliveries outside the off-stump so that they can practise their strokes.'

Dropping the ball casually on the ground, Ananto walked away.

'What's the matter, aren't you going to bowl?' Anokha asked him.

Ananto shook his head. He remembered what his father had said: cricket was a tightrope walk, missing your footing meant death. He was having to perform that tightrope walk now.

'There's a niggle in my shoulder. I'll do some catching practice instead.'

'They called you here for nothing,' Anokha said with a chuckle.

'So it seems.'

'Not seems, that's the truth. The team has been selected already, you're not in it. The selector from my zone told me this morning.'

Anokha was proven right. Ananto was not even the twelfth man, just one of the three extras. Minter was captaining Australia in Bolan's absence. Winning the toss, he chose to bat. Anokha rattled them with three wickets in the first six overs, but they ended the day on 370 without losing any more. Both Bill Toomey and Charles Conrad completed their double centuries the next morning. Declaring at 460 for 3, Australia grabbed a wicket before lunch, and it was Usmani's. Ananto was sitting on a chair beneath a marquee. Their eyes met for a moment as Usmani was returning, and both of them looked away at the same instant. Usmani had been yorked without scoring.

The under-25 team finished their innings at 114 after three hours. Leslie, a chinaman bowler, took 6 wickets, and the off-spinner Madroff, 3. Neither of them had played a Test yet. Ananto was surprised when Minter applied the follow-on instead of choosing to get some batting practice. Usually everyone preferred to get some extra batting before a Test match. But he learnt from an interview with Minter in next morning's newspaper that the captain had wanted to encourage his promising young spinners with the opportunity for more experience and success, so that they could get into the Test team quickly. He wanted them to play a Test in this very series. 'Read this,' Ananto told Anokha, handing him the newspaper.

Having read it, Anokha said, 'And how did these people treat you? Hate them, Sen. Not just batsmen, hate this lot too. It will keep you on the boil. Wait for the chance to take revenge, then tear them apart when the opportunity comes.'

'Yes, that's what I'll do from now on, I'll hate them.'

But his heart did not echo his words. Right from childhood, he had not learnt to hate. His father had kept him at a distance from that emotion, teaching him only to love. Talent, hard work and a hunger for success were the three things that propelled you to greatness, he would say. Ananto felt his father was right. Hatred could bring success for five overs, ten at most. But an entire career could not be built on it.

He decided to work even harder when he returned to Calcutta.

Usmani and Shammi Sarin started the third day on 7 for no loss. Sarin was stumped off of Madroff for 38 in the over before lunch. Usmani was on 18. The score, 64 for 1. At tea, the under-25 team was on 120 for 4. Leslie took 4 wickets in three overs after tea, in the space of just seven balls. Usmani was on 68. Two wickets in hand, at least twenty-five overs to go. He began waging a war of patience with leg-spinner Jyoti Patel as his partner. Anokha was to bat at number 11. Ananto was surprised not to see him padded up in the players' enclosure. Patel would get out any moment and Anokha would have to go in to bat, but he wasn't even ready.

Ananto went into the dressing room to discover Anokha lying on the long massage table, padded up, his fists gathered on his chest, his eyes shut.

'Desi,' said Ananto.

'Is he out?' Anokha opened his eyes.

'No. But why are you lying here this way?'

'I cannot bear to watch anymore. I ran away from the tension.'

'Hate them, fire yourself up.'

'I hate batsmen, Sen, not bowlers.'

Ananto wanted to laugh at this, and at Anokha's plaintive expression. But since that would've been unsuitable right then, he said gravely, 'Then start hating bowlers too from now on. Don't sit alone, it'll make you even more tense. Come outside.'

About twenty thousand spectators were watching with bated breath as Usmani shielded Patel to battle against leg-spin, googlies and off-spin with the help of extraordinary footwork, judgement and technique. When the umpires lifted the bails, Patel was on 2 and Usmani, on 91. They came back, having saved the match.

Ananto went forward. Usmani was acknowledging the applause with his bat raised. Their eyes met.

'You're a great player,' said Ananto.

'Thanks, but I still can't deal with yorkers,' Usmani said without any elation on his face.

~

Ananto returned to Calcutta on the evening flight. Jibon was waiting at the airport with his car. As soon as they hit Jessore Road, heading towards Nagerbazar, Jibon asked, 'Why didn't they have you in the team?'

'I can't say. I didn't ask anyone about it, what's the point?'

'Still a good idea to know why.'

'The East Zone selector wasn't there. Who was going to speak up for me at the selection meeting? All the other selectors were busy pushing players from their own zones. There was no one to back me.'

'Was Hariharan there?'

'I heard he was coming, but he didn't come. Although it was he who made me join the squad.'

'Cliques. The chairman of the selection committee is in the anti-Hariharan group, and so are the North and Central Zone selectors. If drastic changes are made, and you want to get into the Test team, you'll have to show them in Australia's game against East Zone.'

'What do I have to show?'

'That you cannot be ignored anymore.'

Ananto was silent. After a while Jibon asked, 'What sort of bowlers are Leslie and Madroff?'

'Pretty good. They'll get plenty of wickets in Ranji matches. But not Test-class yet.'

'Really? How did they do so well then?'

'Because none of our batsmen are Test-class either, except Usmani. He was yorked by pace in the first innings. Ambrose's in-swing delivery dipped suddenly. But what a performance in the second innings! The spinners didn't know where to pitch the ball. They're still quite raw. Varde or Pillai or Bhojani will take the seam apart. But for some reason our batsmen became terrorized and surrendered their wickets to Leslie and Madroff. Two foreign spinners wreaking havoc on Indian soil—have you heard of such a thing in the past ten years?'

'Both of them will play in this series though, I think.'

'I doubt it. Bolan isn't a fool. Getting all those wickets in a match like this doesn't mean they're Test-class—' Instead of finishing what he was saying, Ananto screamed.

An old woman had suddenly appeared in the path of the car. Jibon braked hard, managing to stop an inch from her body. A bundle of nerves now, she ran across the road, forcing a taxi coming from the opposite direction to screech to a stop.

Jibon laughed. Ananto frowned at him.

'What's that for?'

'How strange life is. She should have been thrown to the ground, but she crossed the road instead. No one gets what they were meant to get.'

For some reason Ananto felt Jibon was talking about himself. He had been desperate to play Test cricket. That would never be possible now. And Ananto was responsible for this, Ananto and Ananto alone. He would remember this all his life, and surely Jibon wouldn't forget either. Ananto began to brood.

After the car turned right into Dum Dum Road from Nagerbazar, Jibon said, 'What are you moping about?'

'You'll probably never be able to forgive me,' Ananto said suddenly.

'What's that?'

'I know it's because of me that you couldn't fulfil your ambition.'

Ananto looked fearfully at the road again as the car jerked to a stop with a harsh screech of the brake. Had they been about to hit someone else? But there was no one there. Turning towards Jibon, Ananto saw his right arm raised.

'Say that again,' Jibon's voice was calm and cold as steel. 'Say that again and see what this arm can do. One blow will crack your skull.'

Jibon continued driving. Neither of them spoke.

'Jibon is angry with me,' Ananto told his mother during dinner. 'I said something to him on the way back.' Telling her of the conversation, he said, 'I can't forget, Ma, I will never forget. I don't think Jibon can, either.'

'Yes, it isn't possible to forget,' a disturbed Tonima said. 'But Jibon is a sensible boy, and large-hearted too. He knows that an accident can take place any time. No one does it deliberately. Still, I know your conscience keeps pricking you. There's nothing to be done. He loves you like a brother.'

'You know, Ma, when I saw his mangled hand that day I shouted, "You WILL play in the Test team, I will make it happen." I feel wretched when I remember. What impossible things we say when we lose our senses! And yet he can go so far as to hope that India loses a Test so that I get to play.'

'If you want to be freed from your guilt, Antu, fulfil Jibon's wishes, wipe his pain away.'

'How?'

Turning to gaze at her husband's photograph on the wall, Tonima murmured, 'He could have told you.' After a few moments' silence, she added, 'Jibon will play Test cricket through Ananto. That will be your penance. If you win, so will Jibon, through you. Antu, your father used to say that the heart and mind are more important than the body. If those two are fully prepared, they can compensate for being underprepared physically.'

Ananto looked intensely at his mother. 'How strange, I see Baba when I look at you.'

India lost the second Test in Kanpur by an innings and 41 runs. It was a slow wicket with even bounce. Australia had made just one change, replacing Pridham with Irwin. Venkatrangan had taken Bhojani's place in the Indian team.

Bolan didn't hesitate to bat after winning the toss. They pounced on the Indian bowling from the very first over, ending the day at 318 for 3. Rogers made 121, Bolan, 101, and Irwin, 79 not out. Dua took 2 wickets, and Farzand 1.

Australia declared at tea on the second day at 531 for 8. Irwin was run out on 188. Bright remained unbeaten with 51. Kapur took 1 wicket on the second day,

Dharaddhar took 2, and Pushkarna, 1. In the remaining hour and a half India made 56 for 4.

India's innings ended at 112 before lunch, Varde top-scoring with 35. The three pace bowlers: Lawton, Ambrose and Bright shared the wickets. After following on, India ended the day on 176 for 2, Usmani continuing his form to remain not out on 87, and Varde, on 42.

On the fourth day, Usmani got a century in just his second Test within 30 balls, hooking Lawton to the boundary. The close-up of his face on TV showed a flash of satisfaction, followed by a dispassionate nonchalance, as though it was nothing to write home about. He smiled when Varde walked up to him to clap him on the back. But Usmani was yorked by Lawton's very next ball. On the way back to the pavilion, the loathing on his face for his own weakness seemed to ignite even the television screen.

'Ahhh!' Ananto had exclaimed when the ball slipped below his bat. It wasn't a drop in concentration after getting his century, Usmani actually couldn't play yorkers. Many great batsmen have such unexpected chinks in their armour. Maybe the Australians had discovered Usmani's Achilles heel. He could certainly overcome this weakness with practice—it was a matter of anticipation and reflexes.

Varde got out on 92. Pushing the ball to mid-off,

Kapur ran halfway down the pitch before deciding to go back. Varde was stranded. He made a desperate effort to return, throwing himself at the crease. But a direct throw had displaced the stumps already. He stared at Kapur for nearly ten seconds. Ananto wondered whether Varde was paying the price for the comments he had made about Kapur in his book. The run should have been taken easily. Kapur threw his bat around, making 36 off 25 balls before getting out. The procession began after this, the batsmen behaving as though they had left their spines behind. There was no discipline in their performance, as though they would be relieved to get out. India were bowled out for 378 in the last over of the day.

Ananto had to try out his new trousers today. In the evening he left for the tailor's shop at Shyambazar. On the bus the passengers were discussing the Test. He listened closely.

'Is this any way to play? All they want is money, who cares for runs.'

'Any idea how much they get?'

'Fourteen thousand per Test, which means two thousand eight hundred a day, can you imagine? In a poor country like ours, a zero is worth 14,000, and yet they're heroes. It's your hard-earned money and mine that's going into their accounts. What are we getting? Only defeats and humiliation.'

'Think of their audacity, they rejected three clauses before signing the agreement with the Board. What do they think of themselves?'

'Why shouldn't they? They know only too well the Board doesn't have the guts to sack them. There are no other players, how will they even have a team? That's what gives them courage.'

'What rubbish! What do you mean there are no players? How will they identify players with all that politics? There's a bowler right here in Bengal, can't remember his name…'

Ananto froze, waiting to hear the name, pressing his face against the hands with which he was holding the rod.

'Ananto Sen.'

Someone shouted from a corner of the bus. 'Lives right here in Dum Dum. Terrific fast bowler, there's no one as good as him in India right now. What pace, what swing, what control, what fantastic line and length!'

'Yes, that's him. If he doesn't get a chance now, when will he ever get to show what he can do? Remember Shute Banerjee? Got to play just the one Test at the end of his career. He was sidelined only for being a Bengali, and it's the same story even now.'

'Did you notice how they threw their wickets? What a way to lose a Test!'

'The Board should sack the entire team, bring in

fresh blood. What's the worst that can happen, the new team will lose too, just like this one. But at least we'll be rid of the vermin. What sort of example are they setting?'

'I think the Board will act this time.'

'They'll do nothing, the same team will play the third Test in Calcutta. They're announcing the team tonight, you'll see I'm right.'

'They should at least drop Kapur and take Ananto Sen. He's not a bad batsman either.'

'If they wanted him to play they'd have taken him in the under-25 team against Australia. Still, if he can pull off something remarkable in the East Zone match in Jamshedpur maybe there's a chance.'

The man who said this was about thirty-five years old. He seemed to be on his way back from office. Perhaps he used to be a regular at cricket matches earlier, but only had time to read the papers now. Ananto got this impression because the man had looked at him without recognizing him. In fact, no one in the bus had recognized him. 'They'll recognize me after the Jamshedpur match,' he told himself.

7

The East Zone team had been put up at the Tata guest house in Jamshedpur. Ananto and the wicketkeeper Torun Mullick were sharing a room on the ground floor.

'I'm going out, Antu. If anyone asks tell them I'll be back by nine.'

Ananto was leaning against a pillow with his legs spread out, reading a weekly sports magazine he had bought at Howrah Station. There was a report on the second Test, with several photographs.

'Are you having dinner where you're going?'

'How can I come back from my sister's house without having dinner?'

As Torun was about to leave, Ananto said, 'What did you think of the pitch, Torun-da?'

'There's still some grass on it, but tomorrow morning you'll see a bald track. That's how it's been for thirty years now out of fear of the visiting fast bowlers. It'll be the same here. There'll be some life in the wicket for an hour or so, after which it'll be of no help to either pacers or spinners. I'll have less to do.'

'Why do you say that?'

'You think they'll let anything go past them?'

After Torun left, Ananto put the magazine away and lay down, staring at the ceiling. He was depressed at what Torun had just told him. He too had felt the wicket wouldn't help the bowlers. Still he had asked Torun in the hope of hearing something that could make him optimistic. But no such luck.

There was a knock on the door. Who was it now? Niranjan and Swaraj Lenka from Odisha were in the next room. Niranjan had dropped in earlier with some homemade sweets. He could get the ball to swing in both directions, in and out, at medium pace off a good length. He would open the bowling with Ananto. The next visitor was Bolai Chanda, in search of chewing gum.

'Come in,' shouted Ananto, still lying in his bed.

But he shot up at the sight of the person who opened the door slowly and entered hesitantly. A young woman, and behind her, a boy of about twelve.

Ananto was dressed in a T-shirt and shorts. Although it was December the room wasn't cold at all, with the doors and windows being shut. Ananto's first thought was to cover his bare legs, which he did with the bedcover lying at his feet.

'Is this Ananto Sen's room?' She had a clear, unaffected way of speaking. No stiffness in her voice or pose.

'Yes,' Ananto gulped mightily trying to get that one word out. Even at twenty-two, he had never spoken to a woman other than his mother and some elderly people.

'Has he gone out?'

'No.' Ananto was nervous now. He had never imagined an unknown woman turning up in his room suddenly one evening in a place like Jamshedpur and asking for him by his name. So his reaction was not unexpected.

'Can you tell me where he is now?'

'Er…it's me…'

'Oh, you!' she laughed and then composed herself. 'You don't know me, and that's quite natural, considering we're meeting for the first time. My name is Bhromora Samajpati. My father's name is Siddheshwar Samajpati, he works at Telco. Your father Arun Sen was his college friend.'

'Oh yes, I've heard Baba speak of him. He studied at Shibpur Engineering College and then went abroad, didn't he? Please sit down,' Ananto pointed at Torun's bed.

They sat down. Ananto was beginning to relax now. But he still wasn't sure whether he should take his legs out from beneath the bedcover. The boy was watching him curiously.

'I've heard of your father too from mine. He says he hasn't seen another person with such determination, honesty and sharp intellect. If he hadn't given up his job he would have been earning a couple of lakhs a year by now.'

Ananto was pleased by this. His chest seemed to expand with pride. He never had the chance to feel this way about his father. Besides Jibon, no one else he knew would understand the kind of person Arun Sen was. Ananto was filled with gratitude to hear a young woman, who had never even seen his father, speak about him with such respect.

'There's a report about you in a local Bengali newspaper. Gungun has read it. This is my brother, his name is Gungun.'

'My name is not Gungun, it's Siddhartha,' the boy corrected her in annoyance.

'You've said so many things about your father in the interview, it's fascinating. It was after reading it that Gungun—' Bhromora threw a sidelong glance at her brother—'Siddhartha told Baba, your friend's son is coming to play here. So Baba said, see if you can bring him home, I want to meet Arun's son.'

Ananto's heart thumped. Meeting him would mean comparing him with his father, even if not openly. And his father's friend was bound to say, 'Nowhere near as good as Arun.'

Suddenly the door opened to admit Niranjan, who immediately said, 'Oh sorry,' and rushed out.

Ananto felt uncomfortable at Niranjan's hasty retreat. He must have thought I'm talking to a fan or a girlfriend, and he shouldn't be here. But Ananto didn't think he was famous enough to have fans.

'Baba has requested you to visit us at home, so has Ma.'

'But…' Ananto was hesitating. Bhromora seemed to be three or four years younger than him. She was dressed in a salwar-kameez and had a fuzzy silk shawl wrapped around herself. Of middling complexion and height, she had a heart-shaped but strong face, bright, restless eyes, hair as short as a boy's, a sharp nose, thick eyebrows, and no ornaments except a watch. No sign of make-up. She was polite but lively.

'But what? Is there a problem? Unless it's because the match starts tomorrow…' Bhromora paused. Ananto looked at her questioningly.

'I believe players prefer to be alone so that they can concentrate.'

Ananto laughed.

'On the contrary, being with people is a relief. I've been trying to get rid of the tension all evening, so you've arrived like with an angel with your proposal.

The only thing is, I must take permission from the manager.'

Throwing the bedcover aside, Ananto got out of bed. Bhromora quickly picked up the sports magazine and lowered her eyes to its pages. Ananto went behind the two of them, put on his jeans, and sneaked a quick look at himself in the mirror.

'I'll be back in a minute.'

Bhaben Mohanty, the manager, was talking to some people in his room on the first floor. The snatches of the conversation that Ananto overheard made it obvious the visitors were pleading for complimentary tickets. Mohanty was a gentle, soft-spoken person. Giving Ananto permission, he said, 'Just don't forget you have to be a hundred per cent fit tomorrow.'

'I will be. Can the players have guests to watch the match?'

Mohanty was perturbed. Throwing a glance at his visitors he said, 'We'll talk later. I don't have any tickets right now.'

'Let's go,' said Ananto, going back to his room. 'By the way, I'd like to return early, preferably by nine o'clock.'

'I'll bring you back.' Bhromora rose to her feet. 'Baba was saying you'd want to go to bed early with a match tomorrow.'

There was an old Fiat waiting outside. Bhromora held

open the door to the seat next to the driver's. Ananto got in, whereupon she walked around the car and got into the driver's seat. Siddhartha got in at the back.

'So tall!' exclaimed Bhromora's mother Mrinal as soon as Ananto straightened after touching her feet.

'Just like his father,' said Siddheshwar.

Overwhelmed by his memories upon seeing Ananto, he was still under the spell, reliving his college days. He kept telling stories about his friendship with Arun Sen, which made Ananto feel increasingly comfortable. He found Siddheshwar large-hearted, cheerful, and dignified, while Mrinal appeared simple and absorbed in her family. He was soon at ease.

'Baba once told me, one lakh rupees isn't essential to my life, what's essential is that I like myself.'

Siddheshwar looked at his wife and children with shining eyes. 'Did you hear that?' he said proudly. 'Isn't this what I used to say about Arun?'

'It's very difficult,' said Bhromora. 'To like oneself, to respect oneself—it's not possible unless one is absolutely clean.'

'Any ideal is bound to be at a height, seemingly out of reach,' said Ananto. 'But that doesn't mean giving up. You have to keep trying, and that's almost a battle. A battle with oneself, isn't that right, Kaka-babu?'

'Not just with oneself, but with others too, and only when you win will you like yourself. If you can put in a superlative performance in this game, what your father said will come true.'

'You must have dinner before you leave, Ananto.' He had assumed Mrinal would make this request. Nodding, he said, 'I'm a small eater though.'

Siddhartha sat next to Ananto at the dining table. He hadn't chatted with the boy yet, but he should, he decided.

'Do you play cricket?'

'Hmm.'

'Gungun is obsessed with cricket. There's nothing else he does other than playing, putting up pictures all over the wall and reading books on cricket,' complained Mrinal affectionately, arranging the bowls of food on the table.

'He's come first in the school cricket quiz,' Siddheshwar said. Siddhartha looked down at his plate in embarrassment.

'Really?'

'Rice or ruti for dinner, which do you prefer?'

'Ruti, please. All right Gungun, no, Siddhartha, I'll ask some questions, can you answer them?'

Siddhartha looked at Ananto doubtfully and nodded.

'Okay, India has never played a Test against South Africa, but an Indian has. Who was he?'

Siddhartha's eyes flashed. 'Duleep Singh,' he

answered gravely. 'He played for England against South Africa. I don't remember the year though.'

'In 1929. All right, now tell me, what's a high-five?'

Siddhartha shook his head. He didn't know.

'You must have seen on TV how the West Indians slap one another on the palm on getting a wicket. That's a high-five. It started in American basketball.'

Ananto thought the cauliflower was delicious. Helping himself to a little more, he said, 'All right, what's a trimmer?'

Siddhartha shook his head again.

'It's the name for a brilliant fast ball, one that misses the stumps by a whisker.'

'You're a fast bowler, Ananto, aren't you?' asked Siddheshwar.

'Yes, I am.'

'Then we'll see your trimmers.'

'I'll try. Are you coming to watch the match?'

'No, I have to go to Calcutta in the morning. Gungun's going. He asked for a ticket as soon as the fixtures were announced.'

'What about the rest of you?'

'No, I don't like sitting there for six hours. You haven't tried the chicken.'

'No Kakima, the cauliflower's so good, that's all I'm going to have. I like vegetarian food.' He looked at Bhromora.

'I have Baba's complimentary ticket. But I haven't decided whether to go to the stadium or watch on TV.'

'Ask me more questions,' pleaded Siddhartha. He wanted to impress his friends with a new bank of knowledge.

After a few moments' thought Ananto said, 'In cricket the number 111 is considered as inauspicious as unlucky thirteen, and is called the Nelson. Why Nelson?'

Everyone looked curiously at Ananto. He knew quite well that Siddhartha wouldn't be able to answer. Looking at Bhromora, he said, 'What about you? You don't have to know cricket to answer this.'

Bhromora's face reddened. She shook her head.

'Nelson is the famous Admiral Nelson of Britain. The British believe one of his arms, one of his legs, and one of his eyes were inoperative. So, 111 is considered unlucky. The funny thing is, Nelson did lose one eye and one arm, but both his legs were intact.'

'May I ask a question? You don't have to know cricket to answer this.'

Ananto realized from Bhromora's voice that she wanted revenge and he wouldn't be able to answer.'

'All right.'

'In which year did Sunday become a weekly holiday in India?'

'Stumped.'

'In 1843. All right, tell me, how much does the American President earn?'

'Bowled out.'

'Two hundred thousand dollars a year. Now tell me, India is considered the second country to have broadcast a satellite-based standard time signal service. Which was the first?'

'Run out.'

'The USA. What's the Indian satellite called?'

'Caught off bat-and-pad.'

'INSAT 1B. All right, one more, this one's about sports, you should know this one.' Bhromora sucked the remnants of food off her fingertips with great attention. 'In which sport does the winning team go backwards?'

Ananto began to ponder and, unable to answer, smiled like a fool at Bhromora.

'What sort of dismissal this time?'

'Timed out. Is there really a sport where the winner goes backwards?'

'Rowing and tug-of-war.'

'I'm an idiot.'

'Some more?'

'No, please declare your innings now, I can't field anymore.'

Bhromora was driving Ananto back to the guest house. Siddhartha was in the backseat.

'Did you get angry?'

'How can such a young boy answer such difficult questions? And why did you say you don't have to know cricket to answer this? There are millions of quiz questions, can one person answer them all?'

Ananto was silent. Leaning forward from the backseat, Siddhartha said, 'Will you give me some more questions?'

'I will. Later.'

'Will you get me autographs from the Australian players?'

'Gungun, stop!' Bhromora scolded him. 'Haven't I told you it's a silly hobby? Instead of getting other people's autographs try to ensure they ask for yours. Put your efforts into becoming a hero yourself.'

Ananto was amazed to hear this. She seemed to be talking like his father. He felt not just respect but also awe.

'Where do you study?'

'Jadavpur University, I'm doing my B.A. My Mashi lives in Hindustan Park, I stay with her.'

'We live in Dum Dum, please visit us, Ma would love to see you.'

'How do you know?'

Ananto was silent. 'I know my mother,' he said in his head.

'I'll go. Come again after the match.'

'I will.'

The car stopped in front of the guest house. Getting out and then leaning forward to lower his face to the window, Ananto said, 'Why don't you come for the first day's play tomorrow?'

'I'll try…all right, I will. Good night.'

'Good night. To you too, Siddhartha.'

Bhromora drove off. Ananto kept looking at the car till it disappeared, before jogging back to his room. He ran into Niranjan outside the door.

'Why did you run away from my room?'

'I thought your…three's a crowd.'

'My father's friend's daughter.'

'Oho. My mistake.'

Ananto opened his door.

'Not going for dinner?'

'No, I ate already.'

He stopped abruptly upon entering his room. Jibon was sitting on his bed.

'Where were you, I've been waiting an hour.'

'Where did you disappear all these days? Kakima said you were in Bangalore on work. But you've been back a week. Where are you staying? Got a ticket?'

'Everything's taken care of. When it's Jamshedpur

I don't have to worry about where to stay or match tickets. What I came to tell you is, you saw the grass on the wicket, didn't you? It's going to be there tomorrow too.'

'What! But Torun-da said they're going to remove it.'

'Torun-da doesn't know. I'm giving you inside information. The Board has given strict instructions. It'll help you.'

'It'll help Lawton, Bright and Ambrose too.'

'So what? You have to look after your interests. Your job is to take wickets, just do it.'

Jibon jumped up.

'You're going?'

'Yes, I'll see you next in Calcutta. I'm not coming here during the game. I'll drive back as soon as the match ends.'

Jibon turned around at the door. 'Did a girl come to see you?'

'Who told you? Must be Niranjan.'

'Doesn't matter who told me. But what's all this? You never did such things before. Are you thinking of yourself as a Test player already? The most vital match of your life starts tomorrow. Try to concentrate, don't let yourself get distracted. Not another word now, go to bed.'

With these peremptory instructions and an admonishing look, Jibon left, slamming the door. A smile spread across Ananto's face. So Jibon wasn't angry or upset with him. He was back to his old form. The same Jibon who had been in his life before.

It was nine-thirty. Torun-da wasn't back yet. Ananto switched off the light and went to bed. He had to concentrate. Useless. A procession of words and faces filed past his eyes. 'So tall!' 'Isn't this what I used to say about Arun?' 'If you can put in a superlative performance in this game, what your father said will come true.' 'I'll try…all right, I will. Good night.'

Sinking into sleep, Ananto sensed Bhaben Mohanty opening the door and drawing his blanket over him.

8

'We were expecting you last evening,' Mrinal complained mildly, her voice brimming with pride.

'There was an official dinner, I had no choice,' Ananto sounded apologetic.

'Of course. Your presence was essential. If the man of the match went missing…'

'…It would be like Kurukshetra without Arjun.'

'Exactly. The last two hours were nothing but Kurukshetra. I couldn't take my eyes off the TV set for a moment—I kept blaming myself for not going to the stadium.' A cloud of regret passed fleetingly across Mrinal's face before the joy returned like sunshine.

'Where's Siddhartha?' asked Ananto.

'He wouldn't have gone out if he'd known you were coming. He'll be back soon, he's gone to meet his friends. If only you could have seen him yesterday—

nothing but Antu-da, as though you're his personal property.'

The phone rang on a shelf in the corner. Bhromora went to answer it.

'Where are you now?… Yes, he's right here…yes, I'll tell him to wait.'

Bhromora came back smiling. 'Gungun has gone looking for you at the guest house. He's asked you to wait for him, he's coming.'

'But I have to leave for Calcutta soon, my friend's driving me back. He had said he would leave yesterday right after the match, but…' Ananto smiled.

'What, how can you leave right now? Aren't you going to have lunch with us?'

'No Kakima, I have to go back with him.'

Mrinal did not insist. All she said was, 'A very close friend?'

'Close doesn't even begin to describe it.'

Ananto told them about Jibon. The scooter accident, stories and incidents from the time his arm was amputated below the wrist, to the time the East Zone team was walking off the grounds after the last ball was bowled in yesterday's match. Both mother and daughter listened with rapt attention.

'Poor boy,' sighed Mrinal. 'What a way to have your dream shattered.'

'The way he takes care of me makes me laugh

sometimes, makes me angry too. Wherever I might be, he watches over what I eat, when I go to bed, whether I'm practising or not. He even knows whom I meet. Just the other day…' Ananto stopped.

They were waiting eagerly for him to tell them more. But he couldn't possibly reveal that Jibon had scolded him for Bhromora's visit. Almost as if to save him from his predicament, four or five boys ran in, shouting, led by Gungun. Ananto noticed each was carrying a school notebook or a sheet of paper. Only one of them had an autograph book.

'They're here for my autograph,' Ananto told Bhromora with a smile.

'Let them have it.'

'But am I a hero?'

Not understanding, Mrinal looked at both of them questioningly.

'He's needling me, Ma,' explained Bhromora, feigning anger. 'Gungun had wanted autographs, I had told him to become a hero himself and give autographs, not ask for them. He's just returned the compliments.'

'But am I a hero?'

'In a situation where Australia is 85 runs away from winning, someone who takes 8 wickets to snatch victory from the jaws of defeat can probably be called a hero, what do you think, Ma?'

'What are you talking about, Bhromora!'

'Come here, all of you,' Bhromora beckoned the boys. 'Mr Hero is dying to give you autographs.'

Ananto gave them his autograph, in Bangla. One of them requested for four additional autographs, for his friends. They milled around him, probably wanting to talk to him.

'Do you have something to tell me?' Ananto asked them.

'Why did you hit just one six, Uncle?'

'Didn't get another chance, got out the next ball.'

'Did you pray to god when you didn't get wickets in the morning yesterday?'

'No.'

'Do you practise every day?'

'That's not possible. But I exercise every day, and run.'

'Then can I be a fast bowler too if I exercise and run every day?'

The boy's ardent, pleading face melted Ananto's heart. 'You want to be a fast bowler?'

'Yes, like you.'

'Then you must exercise every day, run every day, bowl every day. I'm sure you'll be one.'

'Have you played cricket with rubber balls?'

'When I was your age.'

'Did your father scold you for playing?'

'Never.'

'Will you play for India in Tests?'

'I can't decide that. If I'm selected, I will.'

'Enough,' Mrinal raised her arms to stop them. 'He has to leave for Calcutta now.'

Glancing at his watch, Ananto stood up. 'Jibon must have arrived. We're supposed to have lunch together. I should go now.'

'You've made me so happy. You must do well, you must make India proud of you. Don't forget to visit us whenever you're here next.'

'I'll get the car and drive you to the guest house.'

'I'm coming too,' Gungun jumped up.

When they were near the guest house, Ananto spotted Jibon's Premier from a distance and quickly said, 'Stop please, I want to get off here.'

'You don't want to be dropped at the gate?' Bhromora stopped the car, surprised.

How could Ananto tell her that Jibon would shout at him if he saw his friend being driven to the guest house by a young woman? For all he knew Jibon was sitting in his car.

'I'm in the habit of jogging every day, or I don't work up an appetite. I missed it today, so I'll jog from here.' Ananto was sweating even in December.

As soon as he got out and waved, Bhromora said, 'Wait.'

Ananto walked around the car to her window. Bhromora held out a beautiful leather diary. 'An autograph, for me.'

'What!'

Offering him a pen, Bhromora said, 'I have some friends in Calcutta too. I have to show off, haven't I?'

Ananto leafed through the pages of the diary before signing. There were entries in English and Bengali, in perfect handwriting.

'No, don't look. It's personal.'

'I didn't read anything.'

'Write a line or two, and don't forget your address.'

'What should I write?'

'Anything that comes to mind.'

Returning the diary, Ananto raced towards the guest house, as though he was running away. Bhromora opened the diary to see what he had written: 'Be there for every match I play.'

'What's he written, Didi?' Gungun leaned over her shoulder. 'Nothing,' said Bhromora, turning the key in the ignition.

Jibon was lying on Ananto's bed. Torun was still asleep on the other one. Ananto had returned before ten o'clock last night, he had no idea how long the celebrations had continued.

'I've packed all your things, but check for yourself, and tell the manager you're leaving. If we have lunch now and leave we'll be back by seven or seven-thirty.'

After driving for an hour, Jibon said, 'I still can't believe it.'

Ananto smiled. 'Nor can I.'

'They didn't take the match seriously. Despite the green top Bolan didn't include Lawton or Bright. He probably thought the spinners would win it for them again.'

'But other than Leslie and Madroff, it was the same team that played the second Test.'

'That's why I can't believe it. How did you blow away their entire Test batting line-up?'

Ananto smiled. He was looking exhausted, worn-out. 'That's true, how did I? Let me think about it.'

Ananto leaned back and closed his eyes.

9

Bolan had opted to field after winning the toss against the East Zone captain Rahul Sharma. Steele opened the bowling with Ambrose, who sent the openers back to the dressing room in the first four overs, both of them LBW. Because the pavilion was square off the wicket. Ananto couldn't make out the movement of the ball, but he could see the bounce and pace in the wicket. 'What do you think Torun-da, will you have to work harder?' he whispered to the wicket-keeper seated next to him. 'This isn't a bald wicket, plenty of hair on it.'

'So I see. This match will end in two days. I've never seen such a wicket in the seven years I've been playing Ranji matches. Innings defeat.'

'We might win too.'

Torun raised his eyebrows and curled his lips. 'Pad up, you're at number 7.'

Putting on 45 for the third wicket and 40 for the

fourth, East Zone were on 121 for 6 at tea. Ananto was on 2. As he was walking back to the dressing room, he spotted Bhromora coming out of the enclosure for complimentary ticket-holders. She nodded at him. Ananto stopped near the fence.

'So you did find the time.'

'I came after lunch, leaving now.'

'Why not wait till I get out?'

That was what Bhromora did. But she had to wait almost till the end of the first day's play. The East Zone innings ended exactly an hour after tea, after adding another 80 runs, 65 of which came from Ananto. With five sixes, five fours, and a flawless innings over 41 deliveries, he remained not out on 67. No one had thought that East Zone would make 201. Nor had they imagined that Australia would lose both Rogers and Bolan in the first twenty minutes with their total on 25. Ananto took both the wickets in his first 22 balls, having Rogers caught at gully and Bolan at deep square leg.

He had noticed Bhromora and Jibon too. Bhromora did not rise from her chair, only nodding at him, and Jibon was watching her gravely.

Rubbing cream into his face that night, Torun said, 'Don't make your bouncers lift so much, Antu. The batsman didn't have to duck, and even I couldn't stop one of them, it was so high. You have a slower bouncer, it'll be very useful if you can mix it up.'

The second day began dramatically. Ananto's fourth over was unfinished overnight, with 2 balls to go. Minter joined Irwin at the crease, and missed the line of the last ball of Ananto's over. From 25 for 3, Irwin, Woodford and Toomey took the score to 105 for 5 at lunch. Woodford was run out, while Toomey was caught behind off Niranjan. Ananto bowled another eleven overs but got no further wickets.

After lunch Australia stepped up the pace and began to lose wickets too. Niranjan got his second, and Sharma had Pridham caught at slip with his off-break. Ananto started his third spell twenty minutes before tea, with figures of 19-4-51-3. As he was walking to the end of his run-up on the northern side, gazing at the Dolma Hills with a gentle breeze playing on his face, and wondering whether to start with a yorker or an off-cutter, someone screamed, 'Flatten them, Ananto Sen!'

Ananto jumped out of his skin. The wooden galleries were covered by a marquee, the shade making it impossible to identify anyone from the ground. The voice was similar to his father's. His heart began to beat faster, an electric current seemed to run though his head.

Stepping back to play the impossibly fast out-swinger, Irwin couldn't get his bat to it. The ball grazed the off-stump before landing in Torun's gloves. Irwin, who had made over 3,000 runs and taken almost 300 wickets in seventy-three Tests, stared at the pitch. The close in-fielders jumped with their arms in the air. Ananto delivered the next ball with the same motion. It was almost identical to the previous one, hitting the same spot, but much slower. As before, Irwin went on the back foot, and as before, the ball slipped past his bat, this time taking the off-stump bail with it. Irwin turned to glare at Ananto on his way back. His jaws were set now. He took the remaining 2 wickets off the fourth and last balls of the over, caught behind and bowled. He had taken 6 for 51.

'No chance of an innings defeat anymore, it's going to be a draw,' said Torun in the dressing room. 'We can go on till tea tomorrow if we bat patiently.'

East Zone started its second innings after tea trailing by 19 runs. Ambrose and Irwin turned into hurricanes and tore them apart in an hour and a half. Irwin had taken the first 5 wickets all by himself for 31 when Ananto went out to bat. Ambrose had given away 12 runs in eight overs without taking a wicket. Both of Madroff's overs were maidens.

The first ball was a bouncer. Ananto hooked and it went for a six.

'Sixer…sixer…we want sixer.' The cry began on one side of the ground and then spread like multiplication tables being chanted. 'We want sixer…we want sixer…'

Ananto lost his head. They would be happy, he

would make them happy. Irwin was furious with him, he would bowl another bouncer, he was bound to. Ananto prepared to play another hook. It was a slow, straight full-toss. As soon as he heard the sound of the ball hitting the wicket after he had swung and missed, Ananto started walking without looking back. He heard Irwin say something unintelligible and laugh. Ananto's jaws stiffened. He wouldn't make such a stupid mistake ever again in his life.

East Zone were 71 for 8 at the end of the day's play. A sullen Ananto didn't look around or talk to anyone, returning to his room and going straight to bed. Irwin's mocking laughter rang in his ears.

East Zone ended their innings on 103 on the third day. Australia needed 85 to win. They had time enough to get 200.

East Zone were going out to field, Ananto behind everyone else. He heard a stray comment: 'Twenty overs at most. They'll bat like a one-day game.'

He saw Bhromora. She was shaking her fists, signalling to him to fight. A target of 85 was a walk in the park for the Australian batsmen, six of whom were regular Test players. How would he fight? Still, he was happy to see Bhromora's anxious eagerness. Ananto smiled, but as he looked away, he froze.

Jibon. The right sleeve of his kurta was rolled up. The prosthetic was not in its place. A hint of bone at the spot where the arm had tapered off about five inches below the elbow. Jibon was staring at him.

For a moment, there was darkness around Ananto. The Keenan Stadium and the spectators numbering several thousands disappeared from view. The rest of the team was on the ground. Ananto ran to catch up.

The openers took 24 off his first two overs. He was taking East Zone towards a quick defeat with his awry bowling. Sharma replaced him with Satinder. They were scoring 2 or 3 runs per over effortlessly. The Australian victory ship was sailing smoothly on a calm sea.

'Do you hate yourself right now, Antu?'

'Yes, Baba. No bowler likes to be exiled to the long-leg boundary after two overs.'

'Then why aren't you doing what's necessary to like yourself again? Ask for the ball, try to get them out. Haven't I told you one must be hungry for success? You must dream of winning all the time. Go on, try once more. Stay calm. Go, Antu. You can do it. Don't accept defeat before the last ball is bowled. They still need 46 runs. Don't let them get those runs. I'm suffering to see you as a spectator in a corner of the field, Antu. I'm suffering, Antu…'

'Rahul-da!'

From long-leg Ananto ran up to the captain, who was setting the field for his own bowling. He frowned as Ananto charged up madly.

'Let me bowl, Rahul-da. We're losing anyway, give me a couple of overs.'

Ananto pleaded with his clasped hands. After a moment's thought, Sharma said, 'Yes, we've lost already—all right, you can bowl.' Rogers edged a low catch to Barua at second slip off the fifth ball of the over. Diving to his left, Barua couldn't hold the ball but knocked it up in the air for Sharma at first slip to catch it. The sixth ball, a blindingly fast yorker, hit the base of Irwin's middle-stump. There was perfunctory applause in the stadium. Irwin departed, his head bowed.

Niranjan gave away 3 runs in the next over.

Ananto was bowling again. Eight fielders surrounded Bolan. Ananto was on a hat-trick. A straight ball with all his force behind it. He would have to beat Bolan with sheer pace. Ananto was sunk in thought as he walked to the top of his bowling mark.

'Stay calm, Ananto. Don't lose sight of your target trying to bowl fast. Bolan is an accomplished batsman. Use your brains.'

When Bolan realized that the delivery was much slower than Ananto's usual pace and outside the off-stump, he shifted his balance from the back foot to the front and leaned forward for a defensive stroke. The off-cutter found a path between the bat and the pad.

Torun was the first to leap in the air. Running up to

Ananto like a madman, he flung his arms around him and wrestled him to the ground.

'Hat-trick, hat-trick…we're winning, my heart says we're winning.'

The spectators' screams pierced the sky. Everyone wanted to hug him. Ananto's eyes were blank. Nothing made a mark on him.

Possibly on Bolan's instructions, the next batsman swung his bat at everything, hoping to hit Ananto out of the firing line. After two successive boundaries through midwicket, he swung at the fourth delivery too, skying the ball towards mid-off. With no fielder there, Ananto twisted his body from the follow-through and ran for the catch, diving to scoop the ball up inches from the ground with his right hand.

'I'm trying, Baba,' Ananto said to himself, throwing the ball up in the air.

The last ball of the over. The batsman played a strong forward push, the ball racing past Ananto. He gave chase, as did the fielder at cover.

After the first run, the striker, now at the bowler's end, hesitated a moment about running a second before leaving his crease. Ananto had the ball in his hand by now. The batsman was still two yards short of the crease when his 45-yard throw reached the wicketkeeper's gloves.

After cheering for two minutes, the stadium

suddenly fell silent. There was a hint of the unexpected, of the unbelievable. People held their breaths, their heartbeats loud in their ears. Australia needed 34 runs with 5 wickets in hand.

Niranjan to bowl. Two strokes yielded a boundary and then three runs.

Ananto again. Three successive trimmers, beating both the bat and the stumps. The fourth was edged through the slips for a single. Sharma had set an attacking field, with no one on the third-man fence. Barua ran from slip to stop the next edge on the boundary line. Three runs. The batsman blocked the next two deliveries.

Niranjan's over. Both the batsmen had decided to play out Ananto and gather the runs needed to win off the other bowler as quickly as possible. But Niranjan was bowling a good length and line. Unable to score, the batsman became restive and tried to flick a good-length delivery. Eight fielders appealed for LBW, and the umpire raised his finger. Feigning surprise, the batsman pointed to his pad, but the umpire was unmoved. He was used to such demonstrations.

Australia had to get 24 runs with four wickets in hand. Some sort of terror gripped their heart, making the rest of the batsmen abandon both patience and judgement. Ananto was death personified, every ball a summons to annihilation. East Zone had got rid of the cream of the batting, all that remained were the dregs. The stadium was vibrating with tension.

The game ended abruptly. Goldie had come in at number 8. After he had hit Ananto for two sixes over long-on, Sharma stationed a fielder there and told Ananto, 'Bowl a yorker, the slower one.'

Which was exactly what Ananto did. Flattening two of Goldie's stumps, and then getting Levin to hole out at mid-on, also off a slower ball, he took Australia to the edge between defeat and victory. Leslie came in at number 10 and was clean-bowled off the last ball of the over, beaten by sheer pace. One more wicket to go, 12 runs to score.

Neither batting nor bowling was easy at this point. Phelps versus Niranjan—who would win the war of nerves? Many in the pavilion and the gallery had already lost theirs. A number of people were looking away, unable to bear the strain. Silence reigned over the ground.

Niranjan won eventually. Phelps had only managed to take 2 runs from a push to deep mid-wicket. Ten runs to go, Ananto to bowl.

'You've built your castle in the air, Antu. This match will lead you to Test cricket. Your dream is about to come to true. But the castle in the air will collapse if you don't build its foundations now. Take this wicket, that's all you need to do.'

Seeing the ball rising chest-high, Madroff fended it off with his bat. It looped up in the air, descending lazily near Ananto's head. He made no mistake. Australia lost by 9 runs.

10

Jibon had visited Ananto at home after the first day's play of the first Test in Delhi. 'The Board must mean business,' Ananto had said, referring to the report in the newspaper.

'You think the Board will dare touch them after today's performance?' Jibon had said. 'The Board can't take any action if they don't lose. Maybe they're waiting for the right time, and perhaps that time is now.'

The right time was imminent after the losses in Delhi and Kanpur. The results of the games in Hyderabad and Jamshedpur gave courage to the Board. Countrywide condemnation of the players' performance and the criticism in the press put pressure on them to take some action at once. The President of the Board had been waiting for just such an opportunity.

Makarand Varde was informed through a letter on the morning of the first day of the third Test in Calcutta that no member of the team would be allowed to write in the newspapers during the series.

Varde exploded in anger. His contract with *International Features* gave him five thousand rupees for each of his daily reports on the game. Twenty-five thousand from one Test. Imagine giving that up.

'Will I have to answer the questions of ignorant and foolish journalists in press conferences every day from now on? I will explain a nuance in a thousand words, which they will turn into ten lines, some of them not even that, many of them will write just the opposite. Instead of misinformation in fifty newspapers around the country, it would be much more useful if my column appeared in seven or eight papers. People have to be told about the way Bolan is putting pressure on the umpires and the Indian Board, about the way they're making meaningless appeals on the field and threatening the umpires. If we cannot unmask them the pressure will be on us.'

He was talking to journalists, who promptly took it all down. When one of them quoted Varde to Hariharan, he said, 'That's all very well, but those who have reached the stage of playing Test cricket are not children, all of them are mature adults. They're not influenced by what they read in the newspapers. And besides, if the national press edits Varde's comments, or does not understand the main points, let him give a written statement. The CAB has offered a stenographer; Varde can dictate his statement, and it can be typed out, photocopied and distributed to journalists. Isn't this a better method than a column that appears in a handful of papers? Moreover, as the captain, can he really judge his players fairly? That would be unethical, and it would create resentment in the team. What's the point of a column?'

Varde said it would not be possible for him to comply with the instructions of the Board.

Four of the players in the team had deals with four newspapers. They would speak about the game every day, since they could not write. It would appear under their names, for which they would be paid between five hundred and two thousand rupees a day, depending on their popularity. They too gave statements supporting Varde. A tense atmosphere was created in the Indian dressing room. Varde went out for the toss and decided to bat after winning it.

The 85,000 spectators in the stands were stunned by the first ball. Pillai was caught behind, trying to casually cut an enormous out-swinger from Lawton. Then Bright and Lawton sent Varde, Usmani and Nabar back to the pavilion as well. India were 45 for 5 at lunch, and 63 for 6 soon afterwards. Kapur took the battle to the enemy's camp, plundering 24 off two overs from Bright. He made 44 off 88 deliveries, with eight boundaries. Gupta made 69, and Venkatrangan, 49. India were 231 for 8 at the end of the day's play.

Ananto was on his way back home in Jibon's car an hour later. Talking about the game, Jibon said, 'Didn't I tell you after the second Test this team can't win a single Test in this series? You'll see. All of them are disturbed, there's no such thing as team spirit. All they're interested in is how to make some money. Narayan-da said the Board officials are meeting on the rest day in the CAB President's chamber.'

'That's a regular feature.'

'This time it's about the squad for the fourth Test in Bangalore. They're announcing the team on the fifth day.'

'Why will they discuss the squad?' Ananto asked in surprise. 'They're not the selectors.'

'They're the godfathers of the selectors. There will be a selection meeting too, but only to discuss the list provided by the Board.' Jibon stole a look at Ananto. Then, changing the subject, he said, 'Tell Kakima it's been ages since I had her alur dom. Bring some tomorrow.'

'Are you getting the kosha mangsho again?'

'Vegetarian food tomorrow. Mutton the day after. See if you can get some of that kanchagolla at that shop near your house.'

On the second day India added just 10 runs to get

all out at 241. Before that Bright got his 200th Test wicket, in his 46th Test. Kapur had Rogers LBW when Australia was at 32. Then he dismissed Bolan with an incredible out-swinger, Gupta diving in front of first slip to take the catch. Dua and Farzand took a wicket each, and in his second spell Kapur gave Australia another jolt, with Usmani catching Irwin at short fine leg. Kapur had got rid of three batsmen in the space of just seventeen balls, giving away only one run. Australia were 88 for 5. India had struck back, after being in a similar situation on the first day.

The 90,000-odd inspired spectators at Eden Gardens were in full-throated flow now. It was hard to keep one's cool amidst the roars in that huge bowl of a stadium. But Minter, the only recognized batsman left, did just that, supported by Lawton, who was finally out LBW for 54 in the last over of the day off Dharaddhar. It was his second half-century in the series.

With a limited bowling armoury, Varde could not contain Lawton. He helped add 87 runs for the sixth wicket in two hours, and this was the turning point. Minter remained at the crease with 55, a symbol of doggedness. Australia were 179 for 6 at the end of the second day's play. The battle lines were clearly drawn.

Disaster struck on the third day. The spinners bowled with their imaginations and improvizational skills left behind in the dressing room. The fielding was slack. The match kept slipping out of India's grasp.

Despite losing two partners at 213, Minter completed his tenth Test century, remaining not out eventually on 170 from nearly 500 minutes at the crease. And Bright got his highest score in first-class cricket, 68, putting on 161 with Minter for the ninth wicket. The score was 213 for 8 when he came to the crease, and India thought they could finish the Australian innings quickly. But they had not accounted for Bright's batting prowess or his mental toughness. The miraculously-revived Australian innings ended at 381. Kapur took 4 for 91 off 35 overs, and Dharaddhar, 3 for 80.

The first four batsmen in India's second innings returned to the dressing room with the score at 14, 29, 33 and 33, respectively. Ambrose began the destruction. Three batsmen were bowled, beaten by sheer pace. Pillai had thrown his bat around for 20 runs. Pushkarna scored a second duck and earned himself a pair. India was on 36 for 4 at the end of the third day. It could safely be said that Australia had wrapped up both the game and the series. They were 104 ahead, and were still to play their second innings, while India had only 6 wickets in hand.

Every newspaper made the same prediction in its report, stating that the match would end on the fourth day unless there was an earthquake, or the river flooded the entire maidan up to Chowringhee, or an American or Russian missile lost its way and landed at Eden Gardens.

11

Tonima had a touch of fever. Ananto didn't go out on the rest day. In the afternoon he went out on the veranda, sat down on a wicker chair, put his feet up on a stool, and lost himself in a novel, losing all awareness of his surroundings.

When Fuli jumped on to the stool and began to rub her head against his leg, he said a couple of times, 'Mmm, don't disturb me, I can't stroke you now…go away.' Then, shutting his book and reaching out to pick her up, he was startled to see Bhromora sitting in a cycle-rickshaw outside the closed gate.

As he jumped to his feet, the stool clattered to the floor and Fuli was thrown off it. Ananto ran towards the gate.

'Today I got proof of how famous you are. As soon as I asked for Ananto Sen's house on Dum Dum Road, half a dozen people gave me directions, straight till the sweet shop, take a left, then a right at the tubewell, go through two crossroads, take a left at the temple…uff! How far has your fame spread, exactly?'

'Ask any rickshaw-wallah at Dum Dum Station, he'll bring you here.' The pride in the young rickshaw-driver's voice was clear.

'Please come in.' The three words managed to break through Ananto's surprised silence.

'Considering the Test match is on, I was wondering whether you'd be home. It's shocking to see the plight this team is in.'

'Yes, it's dug a deep hole for itself.'

They walked across the portico to the veranda. Bhromora stopped as soon as she caught sight of Arun Sen's photograph on the wall.

'My father.'

'I realized at once,' Bhromora said. 'Baba told me about his broad forehead.'

'Ma's got a slight fever, she's in her room.'

Entering his mother's room, Ananto said, 'Look who's here, Ma.'

Closing the book in her hand, Tonima raised her eyes and immediately sat up in her bed.

'I visited their house in Jamshedpur. This is Bhromora.'

Bhromora bent to touch her feet.

'Come, sit down…I've heard of all of you from Antu. I haven't met your father, but Antu's father told me about him. Who picked your name? It reminds me of Bankimchandra's heroines.'

'My grandfather did, my mother's father, but Bankimchandra's heroine was named Bhromor, mine's Bhromora. My mother's name is Mrinal.'

'Antu, ask Pishi for some tea.'

'Just tea, please. No, I'm not being polite, I had lunch only two hours ago at my aunt's house. She's a doctor, the nursing home she works at is near the station here. So I thought of paying a visit since I was in the neighbourhood.'

'Did you have trouble finding the house? It was quite deserted here when we bought it, very few people. But houses have come up very quickly in the past two years.'

They went out into the veranda, talking about various things over their cups of tea. 'What do you plan to do after you graduate?' Tonima asked.

'I'm going into business.'

Two pairs of eyebrows, the son's and the mother's, shot upwards.

'What sort of business, will you sell saris? I see many educated housewives going from house to house to sell saris. Good idea.' Tonima added, 'I coach students. Same thing.'

'I'm thinking of starting a newspaper for advertisements. Four pages to begin with. It'll have ads from shops in areas like Ballygunge, Gariahat,

Kalighat, Bhabanipur…A free paper, I'll start by distributing say five thousand copies in those localities. Besides the advertisements there'll be news about local events, cultural programmes, schools and colleges in the area, and famous people who live there.'

'Free!' said Ananto in surprise. 'How will you cover your costs then?' He could not tell whether a business like this was viable, and one run by a woman, at that.

'Have you any idea how many shops for jewellery or clothes or shoes or medicines there are in those areas? How many restaurants, nursing homes, beauty parlours, repair shops? All of them will advertise. That will pay for all the costs and help make some profits. There are newspapers like this in America. In Delhi too. A lady has set it up, an eight-page paper, she distributes ten thousand copies. And she's making money, because advertisers have had a good response from customers. Calcutta is also turning into a consumerist society. People are spending more money. That's why three of us have decided to go in for this. In any case, we won't know how it works till we've tried it out.'

'You'll have to work very hard.' Tonima wasn't taking this young woman lightly anymore. She had begun to respect Bhromora for her intelligence, imagination and courage. Bhromora was from an affluent, established family, she would easily find a suitable boy to marry… she was probably good at studies too, and she was attractive if not beautiful. She could have spent a comfortable life had she chosen to get married, but she had opted to struggle instead. She was truly a modern woman, felt Tonima.

'Of course we will. Something like this will never be successful without hard work.' Bhromora said this as though it was as obvious as the fact that the sun rose every morning. 'We'll have to be on the road five or six hours every day, maybe longer.'

'What do your parents think about it?'

'Baba got very excited when he heard.'

'Antu's father was the same. I like your plan too. I would have asked to be a partner if I could have.'

'But first I have to start the whole thing.' Still speaking, Bhromora drew her legs up on her chair. 'Scat, go!' she exclaimed.

Fuli was rubbing her head on Bhromora's leg, but Bhromora wasn't fond of cats. Ananto picked Fuli up. The conversation inevitably turned to cricket.

'Did you go to Eden Gardens?' Ananto asked.

'No chance. I can't bear to sit in front of the TV either for such a long time. But I know we're losing tomorrow.'

Tonima smiled wanly. 'If they'd been like you they wouldn't have been in this situation.'

'Not me, if they'd been like him,' Bhromora looked at Ananto. His ears reddened.

'You'd have known if you'd been at the stadium that

day, Kakima. He did the impossible. It's so thrilling how he snatched the match away from Australia when they were strolling to a victory.'

Tonima looked at her son fondly. Ananto stammered out a response which nobody but Fuli understood. She purred on his lap.

'Performances like these can really inspire people. They make us realize how far a person's determination and ability can take them, isn't that right, Kakima?'

'Antu said you talk the way his father used to, I can see he was right.'

'Really?' Bhromora smiled.

'He used to say you can't achieve anything without a dream. Boys and girls these days have the courage to dream, they've realized that they have to chase their dream, which needs patience and hard work. Antu works hard, he has the hunger too. If he can inspire people he will get the best rewards that life can offer.'

'But Ma, I'm also inspired by her idea of going into business.'

'What, are you planning to start a business too?'

'Not a business, bowling. To each his own.'

It was getting dark. Bhromora would have to go back a long way. She took her leave. Ananto was going to walk her to the bus-stop.

'We'll need a lot of help for our paper,' said Bhromora, 'I'm going to ask you for help too.'

'My help! In what way will I be able to help you?'

'With your fame. If you ask some of the advertisers personally on our behalf, they won't be able to say no.'

Ananto laughed loudly. 'I'm not all that famous yet. I'll have to make a name for myself at the Test-level before people pay attention to me. I haven't even played a Test match yet.'

'You will.'

'How do you know?'

'My heart says so.'

Ananto was silent the rest of the way. As she was getting into the bus, he suddenly raised his arm and said, 'I'll play Test cricket.'

12

Usmani was the only one to put up a fight on the fourth day, remaining not out on 30. Lawton took 6 wickets for 37 runs. The Indian innings ended at 94. Australia won by an innings and 46 runs.

Catcalls and invectives rained down from the stands on either side of the clubhouse, along with paper cups and banana and orange peels. A few brickbats too. Torches were lit in different parts of the gallery. Thousands of faces were contorted in rage. The anger was not so much at the defeat as it was at the meek surrender. The doors to the Indian dressing room were shut. Bolan and his men returned from the field with broad smiles. The last two Indian batsmen were spat upon. A ferocious crowd was waiting in front of the clubhouse for the Indian team to emerge in its bus. The police had to use their batons to clear a path for the bus, in which every face at every window looked tired, disappointed, and frustrated. Bricks were thrown at the bus as it drove back to the hotel.

A CAB official appeared in the press box even before India's second innings had ended to announce that the selectors would be meeting now. The Board President had called a press conference in the clubhouse lunch room at 1 p.m. He would announce the team personally.

Informed of this by a reporter, Jibon said, 'I'm staying, Antu, I'll leave only after the names have been announced. Want to go downstairs for a cup of tea?'

Ananto was gazing at the field from the complimentary seats high up in the clubhouse. 'You go,' he said.

Newspapers and orange peel were strewn all over the field. The groundsmen were clearing them. The police were standing around the pitch to protect it. The stands were still full of people, no one was in a hurry to return, it was barely afternoon.

Ananto's eyes were fixed on the field. Hope and despair swept over him in waves. He would know his fate in an hour. Was he going to be included, or was he going to be ignored? 'I'll play Test cricket,' he had declared yesterday. But when?

Even three years ago, he would laugh when the subject came up. 'I'm not being over-ambitious right now. First Bengal, then East Zone…one step at a time.'

But Jibon had already been dreaming of playing

in Tests. Ananto looked up at the sky. It seemed to him that thick clouds were speeding towards him, darkness was closing in, just like they had that day. The treetops were swaying madly. Birds were beating their wings desperately to stop themselves from being blown away. His heart trembled suddenly with an unknown fear.

And then!

Fat drops of rain had begun to fall noisily. Their uncovered bodies were being drenched in gusts of wind and rain. His eyes glittering, Jibon had suddenly held his arms out, screaming 'Yahooooo!' and raced towards the staircase. Kicking the iron door open, he had run into the field, stopping on the grass. Raising his arms towards the sky, he had turned to Ananto.

'Antu, I'm going to play in Tests,' Jibon had shouted. 'Can you hear me, Antu, I'm going to play in Tests. God has sent word that I'll play.'

Everything had become blurred in the rain. Jibon had been rolling around on the field in ecstasy. Ananto had said, 'Jibon will play in Tests one day, take my word for it, Mohon-da.' In the torrential rain he had seen Jibon lying on the ground, facing the sky, his arms spread out. Like an inert dead body. For a moment, Ananto's heart had leapt into his mouth.

'Ahhhh!' Ananto put his hand on his heart and leaned forward. 'You couldn't play in Tests,' he whispered. 'I killed your dreams. Forgive me, Jibon. I can't, I can't. I can't play with this weight on my heart.'

'Antu…Antu…Antu!'

Jibon was running up the stairs like a madman, shouting like a madman too.

'Antu, you—' Jibon tripped on the step and fell on his face.

Ananto ran towards him, anxiously shouting, 'Are you all right?' Jibon's head had struck the cement edge of the stands. He was bleeding from his forehead. Struggling to his feet he ran towards Ananto and almost threw himself into his arms.

'Antuuuuu…'

Burying his face in Anonto's chest, Jibon burst into tears.

'Antu, I was going to play Test cricket…didn't you say, I WAS going to play, that you'd make it happen? Do you remember?'

Jibon raised his face. The blood had flowed down his face and mingled with his tears. There was a profound sense of serenity in his eyes. Ananto's first thought was, this must be what god's face looks like.

'You're in the squad of fourteen, Antu. Panigrahi just announced the names.'

Baba! Ananto's eyes rose towards the sky. His entire body trembled briefly. Controlling himself, he said, 'Come with me at once to the medical unit downstairs.'

'No,' said Jibon childishly. 'Aren't you happy? My dream has been fulfilled, and you're worrying about a tiny cut?' His eyes filled with tears again.

The rows of seats above the clubhouse were empty. The entire gallery around the stadium was deserted. Just two people facing each other. At one point the taller of them knelt slowly, wrapped his arms around the shorter one and leant his head on his chest.

~

The next day the biggest headlines in every newspaper in India were not about India's third successive defeat.

'Indian cricket makes history'.

'Eight players axed from Test team'.

'Indian Cricket Board takes gutsy decision'.

'The Board takes revenge'.

'The Board shows it has a spine'.

And then the news. Most of the reports were replete with words like 'sensational', 'dramatic', 'unimaginable', 'stunning', and so on.

The fourteen-member squad for the fourth Test against Australia announced by the Board President S. Panigrahi does not include eight of the eleven players who played for India in Calcutta, including captain Makarand Varde. The other three are Usmani, Nabar and Venkatrangan. The new captain of India is the current skipper of Gujarat, the 39-year-old Feroze Nawroji Kambatta, who was dropped from the Indian side eight years ago. He has played twenty-two Tests. All the players who had signed their contracts only after rejecting three of the clauses have been dropped. The four young players who had accepted all the terms—Usmani, Nabar, Anokha and Gowda—have been retained in the squad, along with Venkatrangan.

Besides these six players, the others in the squad are two wicket-keepers, Sanjay Shukla (Maharashtra) and Vinay Marathe (Maharashtra), two batsmen, Durga Niranjan (Delhi) and Shammi Sarin (Haryana), two spinners, Tarsem Kumar (Punjab) and Jyoti Patel (Bombay), and two pace bowlers, Farukh Mirza (Hyderabad) and Ananto Sen (Bengal).

The Bangalore Test was due to start in five days. Ananto would leave on the evening flight three days before the game. But before that, reporters and photographs laid siege on him for two days, invading his house from the early hours of the morning till late at night. Journalists from well-known as well as unknown newspapers and magazines, some from the districts, pestered him constantly with ridiculous questions. Eventually Tonima said, 'You'd better spend the day at Jibon's. If they come again I'll tell them you're staying with relatives, you'll be back the day after tomorrow. By that time you'll be in Bangalore.'

'It's a sin to lie, Ma.'

'Sometimes lying is a virtue. This is one of those cases. You need peace and quiet.'

But it was Jibon who turned up Ananto's house instead. When a reporter asked, 'Do you bowl in-swingers or out-swingers?' Jibon answered, 'Neither, he bowls in-spin and out-spin.' The reporter noted this down and Ananto grinned. Then the same reporter asked, 'When do you prefer bowling bouncers?' Before Ananto could answer, Jibon said, 'He makes the ball bounce when he isn't getting a wicket with shooters. You know what shooters are, don't you?' 'Of course I do,' the reporter smiled. 'It's another name for long hops. In cricket it's normal for the same thing to have different names.'

After the reporter left Jibon said, 'Be careful whom you talk to. India has at least 50 million cricket pundits who have never touched a bat or a ball. This was one of them. Don't read what they write about you in the papers. Your blood pressure will shoot up…Listen, I'm going to Bangalore too, I'll get there the day before the match. I've booked a room at the Rama. It's near the stadium. The team will stay at a five-star hotel, the West End. Keep a ticket for me, I'll collect it from your hotel.'

13

It was drizzling when Ananto's plane landed in Bangalore. This was his second visit to the garden city. He had heard it was a clean and beautiful place, full of trees. Several officials of the Karnataka Cricket Association were milling around the airport, two of whom escorted Ananto to the hotel. On the way his curious eyes took in the cricket stadium and landmarks like Cubbon Park, Vidhan Soudha and the Raj Bhavan.

His room was on the first floor. The receptionist informed him that his roommate was Deshraj Anokha, who would arrive the next afternoon from Delhi. The two of them had been thrown together again, the idea being to help the two fast bowlers develop a rapport. All teams did this. The opening batsmen shared a room, as did the spinners. Only the captain and the manager had their rooms to themselves.

Kambatta had arrived that afternoon. Ananto felt

he should make a courtesy call on the captain and introduce himself. He had only seen Kambatta in photographs. Bearded, of middling build, with pale eyes that held a suspicious look. He had 1,072 runs in twenty-two Tests with one century and an average of about 30. In Ranji Trophy matches he had made 5,210 runs with eighteen centuries and an average of 54. He had scored 619 runs and hit four centuries in eight innings in the last season, and had just notched up his third century this season last week. Kambatta was in top form right now.

Ananto had been told that Kambatta was a serious, taciturn man, a stickler for discipline. A coterie within the Board, along with Mridul Sharma, then the captain of the team and now a selector, had conspired to have him dropped. A rumour was floated to the effect that he could not play fast bowlers.

Ananto knocked instead of ringing the bell. 'Come in,' said a deep voice at once. He entered.

It was a medium-sized suite. Kambatta was lying back in a sofa, his feet up on the centre table in the small living room. He was dressed in a Lucknow chikan kurta-pyjama. Seven or eight newspapers were strewn around the table and the sofa, one in his hand. It was clear from the firmness of his shoulders, neck and jaw, and the structure of his chest and arms that he was serious about his fitness.

Ananto bent from the waist in a slightly theatrical bow. Lowering his legs to the floor and sitting up, Kambatta said, 'You're Ananto Sen.'

'Yes, sir.'

'You have the build of a fast bowler, so I had no trouble recognizing you. I only have one real pace bowler in my team…sit down, when did you arrive?'

'Half an hour ago.'

Training his piercing eyes on Ananto for a few moments, Kambatta said, 'We're complete strangers. Most of the team members do not know their skipper. But I don't think that'll be a problem. Because we will be playing with an objective—which is to prove ourselves. This objective will unite us, inspire us too. We have all climbed to the highest rung of cricket now, none of us is immature. So I don't have to give a speech to anyone to ask them to give 100 per cent. All of you have got an unexpected opportunity to establish yourselves—it has come to you in a way you could never have imagined. Back in our days no one could play a Test at twenty-two or twenty-three, unless they were exceptionally talented or had a godfather in the selection committee.'

Ananto noticed a trace of bitterness in Kambatta's voice, which he stifled skilfully. Leaning forward suddenly and holding out his hand, he said, 'Let me see your arm.'

Ananto held his right arm out. Holding it, Kambatta examined his fingers and palms carefully, pressing them with his fingertips.

'Do you do weight-training?'

'Yes, I have the equipment at home.'

'I was astonished by your performance in the East Zone match. Were the Australians not serious about the game?'

'Not at first. But they tried hard when they saw they were about to face their first defeat on the tour.'

'What sort of wicket was it?'

'There was grass on the pitch. Hard surface, with bounce. The kind of wicket I like.'

'Will you be able to show results if you get a similar wicket here?'

This was a tough question. If he said yes he would appear to be an over-confident braggart. But if he hesitated it would suggest a lack of determination, no killer instinct. To say he would try his best would be foolish—obviously he would try his best, or why was he playing Test cricket?

'It depends on a few factors.'

Kambatta sat up straighter. His eyes grew sharper.

'Such as?'

'The confidence of the opposition, the state of the match, the confidence of my own team, whether every catch is being taken, and besides, the wicket and the weather can change character suddenly. Most importantly, my performance will depend on my own mental and physical condition during the match.'

'Did you get all of these in Jamshedpur?'

About to answer, Ananto paused. Bhromora's face flashed before his eyes. But it was instantly replaced by a severed arm. He heard a whisper in his ear. 'I think you're wonderful, Antu. And I'm proud that you're my friend.'

'Yes, I did.'

'And your physical condition now?'

'Perfect, from top to toe.'

The doorbell rang.

'Come in.' Kambatta glanced at the door. Rakesh Khanna, the team manager, and Raghu Rao, the local manager, entered. Introducing Ananto to them, Kambatta said, 'I don't think our problems will be solved just by dealing with Lawton, Bright or Ambrose. We have to create problems for Australia too. You can leave now, Sen. I'm sure you're usually in bed by ten.'

Ananto nodded, bowed to everyone, and left. On his way to the restaurant for dinner, he was struck by a thought. What was that about creating problems for Australia? Was Ananto Sen that problem? Did this mean he was in the team? Was he going to play Test cricket, then?

14

Jibon had come directly to West End after checking in at his own hotel. Taking his ticket from Ananto, he said, 'I've never been here before. It's a good seat, I hope.'

'There's an area just outside the dressing room where the players sit. On its left are eleven or twelve long rows of seats, that's where you are. It's not like Eden Gardens. Anyone can enter the dressing room if they want to. A narrow staircase leads directly into the ground from the first floor. Next to it is the press enclosure.'

'What about the team selection? Tonight or tomorrow morning?'

The bathroom door was open. They could hear the sounds of clothes being washed. Anokha had always been used to washing his own things of daily use— he didn't send his handkerchiefs, sweat-bands, socks, vests or underclothes to the hotel laundry. Apparently he didn't feel comfortable wearing them unless he had washed them himself. So he was at it now with a bar of laundry soap. He would spread them out on the desk and chairs to dry afterwards.

Overhearing Jibon, Anokha shouted from the bathroom, 'The selection meeting is on in the manager's room. I have my sources, I'll get the names of the playing eleven soon.'

Jibon went up to the bathroom door. Anokha was squatting on the floor, dressed in a pair of shorts, scrubbing his clothes. The white marble floor was awash in foam. 'I'll wait for a while then,' said Jibon. 'Are you sure of your sources?'

'The manager himself is my source. Don't worry, Jibon, Sen is certain to be in the team. The way the skipper made him work at the nets these last two days, giving him special attention, all of us are sure he's in.'

'If Antu's in the team I'll send you the same rabri I treated you to in Calcutta, the one from Sharma's.'

'How much?'

'One kilo, two kilos…'

'Then you'd better place a trunk-call to Calcutta tonight and book a kilo of rabri. It must get here by tomorrow's flight.'

Anokha had lightened the mood. The phone rang. Answering, Ananto shouted, 'Anokha, it's for you.'

Anokha jumped up like a spring to answer.

'Yes, I'll be there at once.'

He looked around for his trousers.

Ananto's sweatpants were lying nearby. Slipping them on quickly, he said, 'Khanna is calling me to his room.'

Ananto and Jibon exchanged glances after Anokha went out.

'I'm feeling nervous, Antu.'

'Me too.'

Anokha's two-in-one radio-cum-tape-recorder was lying on his bed. Ananto pressed the play button. The room filled with the screaming vocals and loud drumming of a rock number. Ananto couldn't stand this sort of music, but this battering of noise was soothing his frayed nerves right now.

Jibon glanced at his watch. Ananto looked at the door.

'When will he be back?'

'No idea.'

'What if he says your name's not on the list?'

'What if he does? I won't die.'

'It's very hot, you're sweating.'

'The air-conditioning is on.'

'Turn it up.'

Ananto went up to the regulator.

'You're sweating, Antu, go splash some water on your face.'

'I'm all right.'

'No, listen to me. You'll feel better.'

Despite his reluctance, Ananto slipped on his rubber sandals to go into the bathroom. At that moment the door burst open. Jibon gazed mutely at Anokha, who was standing outside.

'Rabriiiiii....' Anokha shouted, pumping his fists.

'Am I in...?' Ananto's anxious voice floated out of the bathroom, and immediately they heard him slipping and falling on the floor.

'Owwww...Jibon, can you come here?'

'What is it, what's the matter, Antu?' One of Ananto's slippers was lying near the bathtub. He was trying to raise himself to his feet.

'Anokha, Anokha!' Jibon tried to help Ananto up.

Anokha came in. Slapping his forehead, he said, 'Oh my god!' and helped Ananto get to his feet.

'My mistake,' said Anokha remorsefully. 'I should have rinsed the foam off. I got distracted by the phone.'

'It was I who told him to splash some water on his face. That's why he—' Jibon choked.

'What did Khanna say?' Ananto walked slowly to his bed and sat down.

A smile spread across Anokha's face. 'You're in the team, Sen.'

'So you're going to play a Test Match, Antu.' Jibon's eyes were moist.

'Sen, check if you're injured, we must inform the doctor at once.'

'No, don't call the doctor,' Jibon intervened. 'Antu, walk.'

Ananta began to walk around the room. 'The ankles and knees are fine. I fell on my back.' Ananto put his hand on a spot on his spine, below the lumbar region.

'Try bending forward.'

Ananto did. 'Slight pain.'

'Try the follow-through action,' Jibon's voice shook.

Choosing an uncluttered area of the room, Ananto took five quick steps, jumped as though delivering the ball, and leant forward, putting his weight on his left leg.

'Owww!' A stifled cry came from his throat.

'Is it hurting?' Anokha put his hand on Ananto's back. 'You're playing the first Test of your life tomorrow. You can't play unless you're a hundred per cent fit. Try once more, see if it's still hurting.'

'No need to try again,' Jibon exclaimed brusquely. 'Antu's fine, he's a hundred per cent fit.'

'You don't understand, Jibon.'

'I understand very well, Anokha, I used to play cricket too. One night's rest and the pain will be gone. No need to complicate matters by consulting the doctor. Don't call the doctor, Anokha, and don't tell anyone either.'

'Is he going to hide his injury?'

'Yes, he will,' Jibon exploded suddenly. 'How can he be so close and then not play. How can that be possible?'

'But that'll be a big mistake. If the skipper finds out…don't you understand the importance of this match, Jibon? The board has taken a huge risk, and the careers of so many new players depends on this match. Don't you understand these things?'

'I do. But can you explain to me why this happened to Antu in the first place? He wouldn't have been in this situation if you hadn't been careless and left the bathroom floor slippery.'

'Sen, I'm sorry, I'm really terribly sorry. I didn't do it intentionally, you know,' Anokha looked at Ananto miserably.

But Jibon was staring at him through narrowed eyes. Anokha was looking alarmed, his face was drained of blood.

'Do you think I deliberately…'

Jibon looked grim.

'What do you think you're saying, Jibon?' Finally Ananto spoke up. 'You're completely wrong. Anokha is my friend, my well-wisher. He can never do anything dirty. There's nothing wrong with me. This sort of pain is a regular affair. Yesterday I dived for a ball when fielding, hurt my shoulder. I was bowling three minutes later.'

'Then there's no need to call the doctor or tell anyone, Anokha. You heard Ananto say it himself, he isn't injured.'

Anokha had paled at these exchanges. 'All right,' was all he said.

15

Ananto woke up early in the morning, and his first thought was that a new chapter in Jibon's life would begin today. As he tried to get out of bed, a muted groan emerged from his throat. He whipped his head towards Anokha's bed. Anokha was asleep. Ananto used his arms to raise himself to a sitting position. How strangely the chapter was about to begin. Through the window he saw it was drizzling, the sky cloudy.

He had no difficulty walking about, but he could feel the pain. Having paced about the room lightly, he felt a sharp stab of pain in the lower part of his spine as soon as he sat down in his bed. He rose to his feet again, telling himself that some rest, a warm compress, a massage and some painkilling tablets would do the trick. But doing all this would mean letting everyone know. What was more, the hint that Jibon had dropped yesterday had hurt Anokha, leaving him dejected.

But it really wasn't his fault. Ananto would have to

bowl to prove that he was not in pain, so that Anokha could be relieved of his guilt. Or else he would die of remorse. Jibon shouldn't have put this enormous burden on him. In trying to help Ananto, he had ended up making him uncomfortable. Ananto would have to tell him not to say anything more, not to come to the hotel.

The phone rang. Answering the call, Ananto said, 'Ananto Sen speaking.' Jibon asked, 'How's the pain, Antu?'

'Jibon, you were wrong to say all those things to Anokha yesterday.'

'To hell with Anokha. Think of yourself first. Are you still in pain?'

'No.'

'Thank goodness. All night I just…'

Ananto disconnected the call.

'Was that Jibon?'

Startled, Ananto turned around to see Anokha sitting up in his bed.

'No, a friend of mine who lives here. He was calling to congratulate me.'

'Your injury…'

'It's fine. Perfectly all right.'

When Ananto began bowling at the nets, he made sure not to bend. During his run-up he felt as though someone was poking the base of his spine with a red-hot rod. He tried to bowl standing up, without going into a follow through.'

'What's the matter, why are you bowling this way?' Kambatta came up to him. 'Bowl properly.'

'Yes, I was just warming up.'

Delivering the next ball with an eleven-step run-up, Ananto followed up as usual. He grimaced with pain, but he didn't allow a single sound to escape his lips. Usmani was batting. He had played a defensive shot on the back foot. The ball was rolling towards Ananto. He didn't dare bend to pick it up. Stopping it with his foot, he bent at the knee to gather it. Just two people noticed—Anokha, and Jibon, who was sitting in the stands.

The series had lost its attraction after three successive defeats. There were no stars playing either. India were bound to be routed. On top of which the sky was cloudy. It had rained last night, followed by a couple of spells this morning. The game would be disrupted constantly, spectators wouldn't get their money's worth. It would be wiser to stay at home and watch the match on TV. Ticket sales had been low for these reasons. Most of the gallery was empty.

Kambatta won the toss. India would bat. Ananto heaved a sigh of relief. So he wouldn't have to bowl today. He could rest all day—surely India would be able to bat all day? Usmani and Sarin were padded up. Vinay Marathe was the twelfth man. Gowda the off-spinner was a local boy; he and the Mumbai leg-spinner Jyoti Patel were amongst the reserves. The only specialist spinner in the side was Tarsem Kumar from Punjab. Kambatta himself was a good off-break bowler, though. But no one could remember the last time India had played a Test with just one specialist spinner. In the same way, no one could remember when, if ever, India had last played with four pace bowlers—Deshraj Anokha, Ananto Sen, Durga Das and Farooq Mirza.

While the Indian eleven was being announced by the scorer in the press box, one of the journalists said mockingly, so that everyone could hear, 'My god, so many pace bowlers? Has India turned into the West Indies?'

'Is Feroze Nawroji Lloyd our skipper?' quipped another.

'Greenidge and Haynes are going out to bat now. Lawton and Bright will be shred to pieces.'

Bolan and his men were entering the field. Their left-arm spinner Leslie was getting his Test cap. There was some scattered applause as Usmani and Sarin walked in.

Ananto's eyes sought out Jibon. He was seated in the middle of the fourth row from the front. The way in and out of the pavilion went past his seat. Since there was a TV set in the dressing room, Ananto decided to sprawl on a chair and watch the match on it. He wouldn't be able to sit upright outside.

The first two overs were maidens. Kambatta was padded up, resting his chin on his hands, which were clasping his bat, his eyes on the TV set. They didn't reveal what was on his mind. Ananto was sitting behind him.

Seven overs had gone by. Usmani was on 9, having scored two boundaries off Lawton with straight drives. Suddenly a delivery from Bright jumped from the good-length spot. Usmani raised his bat to the level of his face. The ball went to Rogers at short-leg. India had lost its first wicket at 12. Nabar walked in, with Kambatta scheduled to follow him. He went outside. Usmani entered grimly. Sitting on a chair with a brooding expression, he took his pads off after some time.

It was like territorial war. Sarin and Nabar put on 65 runs in 30 overs. Only once did Sarin lose his patience to hook Lawton to the boundary off successive balls, but he withdrew into a shell immediately.

With India on 77, Sarin nicked an off-cutter from Ambrose into Phelps's gloves to be dismissed for 30. Replacing him, Kambatta hooked and on-drove the first two deliveries he faced from Ambrose, picking up a boundary and 3 runs, respectively. The spectators came alive suddenly.

'What do you make of the wicket?' Anokha asked Sarin when he returned.

'Batting wicket. Slow. A little moist. I can't make out how the ball to Usmani jumped so much.'

Nabar came back in the over before tea, edging an Ambrose off-cutter to Phelps behind the wicket, just like Sarin. His 43 was not spectacular, but incomparably useful. India was on 116 for 3. Venkatrangan was dismissed for just 5. Durga Das, an all-rounder, walked in, had a quick conference with Kambatta, and concentrated on a single task—making sure that his partner was on strike. And Kambatta picked the pace bowlers to send a response to his critics. After a glittering innings of 57, he was caught by Leslie in the slips off Lawton. India was 160 for 5.

Now the Indian batting began to reflect its inexperience. Durga Das followed Kambatta into the pavilion with a score of 16, giving Leslie his first Test wicket. Sanjay Shukla scored a duck on debut, and Mirza, 1. All three of them had tried to hit the ball out of the ground. But Ananto tried to get out off the very first ball.

Standing up straight so that he wouldn't have to bend to take a proper stance, Ananto swung at Leslie more or less blindly. The first three balls went for six over the bowler's head. He was stumped off the fourth ball. With a sigh of relief, he walked back past

Kambatta, who was seated in his chair. A quick look at the captain's face revealed flaming rage.

India ended the day on 203 for 9.

—

'Is the team under the impression we're playing an exhibition match?'

Kambatta asked the question coldly, sternly in the dressing room. Silence. Several heads were lowered.

'This is a five-day match, not a one-day game. How many times did I ask you to bat patiently? Not one of you listened. This is no way to play a Test. None of you applied yourself to the task. Aren't any of you ambitious? Do you think you've achieved success by playing a single Test? The Board placed its trust in you and dropped established, well-known players. Is this how you're going to pay them back? Don't you have any self-respect?'

Identifying where each of them had gone wrong, Kambatta turned to Ananto. 'What's wrong with you? Why that batting stance? Are you having trouble bending?'

Ananto shrivelled in fear. 'No,' he stammered, 'I couldn't make out Leslie's flight, so I stood upright.'

'Hmm.'

With a single utterance and a suspicious glance, Kambatta made it clear he didn't believe Ananto.

'Is it hurting very much?' Anokha whispered in the bus on the way back to the hotel. 'You'll have to bowl tomorrow.'

Ananto shrugged. Which could have meant both yes and no.

They filed out of the bus when it stopped at the hotel. Kambatta was directly in front of Ananto. He was wiping his face, a leather bag slung from his shoulder. The handkerchief slipped from his hand as he was stepping off the coach. Ananto was behind him.

'Your kerchief, sir.'

Kambatta was a few steps ahead. He turned around. Bending to pick it up, Ananto groaned in pain and straightened up. Then he bent from the knee to gather the handkerchief.

Taking it, Kambatta said in a steely voice, 'See the doctor at once. Go to your room, I'm coming.'

He strode inside. Ananto made two realizations. Kamabatta had dropped the handkerchief deliberately to check whether he was injured, and that hell awaited him now.

Having examined him, the doctor took him to the hospital for infra-red radiation and gave him a few pills. 'Rest is the only answer,' he said.

Kambatta sent for Ananto as soon as he was back. Rakesh Khanna was sitting there too. Both of them were furious.

'I did not expect such dishonesty from you. Do you know how much you have harmed not just the team but also the nation? Have you forgotten you're playing for the country, not for your club; that you're representing millions?'

Kambatta's voice began to rise. Ananto's head dropped. Khanna was staring at him piercingly.

'You could have told us last night. Even this morning, before the team was submitted. I could have included a fully fit player instead. You're an important part of my plan, now that plan is demolished. Everything is ruined.'

Kambatta was lost in thought, his eyes on the floor. Ananto had almost turned into stone. His blood had stopped flowing, his breath had frozen, even his eyes were still. He had nothing to say. What he had done was unforgiveable. He had no excuse to offer, no explanation. Ananto had never been faced with such humiliation. Nothing but death could rescue him now. But perhaps just to prove that he hadn't become a statue, two teardrops rolled down his cheeks.

'Can you imagine the enormous risk taken to drop the top players to build this team, with faith in youngsters like you? There's been a storm of criticism. But what you have done…you're not a child, Sen. You couldn't resist the temptation of getting a Test cap.'

Kambatta's voice reverberated like the hero's lament in a Greek tragedy. He was pacing up and down, running his hands through his hair. Khanna's eyes followed him around the room.

'Look where greed and ambition can take a man.' What Kambatta was telling himself was clearly audible. 'How long I've waited for this day, how many years! I was going to wipe out all the ink smeared on my reputation and show them I can play pace bowlers. Lawton! Bright! Ambrose! Hah! I'd have won this Test, the wicket will deteriorate constantly. I could have had Australia all out under 150…if this fool hadn't cheated me.'

Ananto couldn't take it anymore. He ran out of the room like a wounded animal chased by predators.

Returning to his room, he saw Anokha on the phone with someone. When he saw Ananto he said into the phone, 'He's here, talk to him.' Anokha held the receiver out to Ananto. 'It's Jibon.'

A wild growl emerged from Ananto's throat. He snatched the phone from Anokha.

'Jibon?'

'Yes, what did Kambatta say?'

'Jibon, you've caused me great harm. You've ruined me. I cannot hold my head up anywhere. I'm a liar, I'm a cheat, I'm greedy…I have hurt millions of people…I have betrayed the nation…every word is true. I have had to accept all of it…you know who's responsible for this…you, nobody but you.'

Ananto was panting. He was foaming at the mouth.

Anokha was looking at him in astonishment. Jibon was silent.

'You know what I think now, why did I have to drive the scooter that day, why did I have to have an accident, why did I blame myself for your injury, why did you say "Antu, I'll never play Test cricket." Why why why…why did you ask me to lie about my injury, I wouldn't have had to face this humiliation. I hate myself now Jibon. How will I face my mother, what will I tell my father's photograph: I have ground into the dust all that you taught me, I have made you hang your head in shame…? I have to kill myself Jibon, suicide…'

Anokha came up to Ananto as soon as he replaced the receiver in its cradle.

'What do you mean "suicide"? Don't even think of all this, Sen. Life is too valuable to throw away so easily. It was I who was responsible for your injury, if I had been careful…what Jibon said yesterday was right.'

Slapping Ananto on his back, Anokha said in a cavalier tone, 'It's just one day yaar, there are four days to go. Watch me bowl tomorrow. I'll stop Australia in their tracks. Don't be upset.'

Ananto lay face down on his bed. Rock music was playing on the tape-recorder, but Ananto couldn't hear a note. Despite Anokha's repeated requests he didn't go for dinner.

After examining him the next morning, the doctor said he couldn't bowl yet, for that would complicate the injury. It was best not to move at all.

'No need to go to the stadium, stay in your room.'

Khanna left with an annoyed expression after giving his instructions. Kambatta hadn't paid a single visit. But everyone else in the team had. Ananto felt their expressions held the same accusation—you have let us down.

Anokha's radio-cum-tape-recorder was lying on the bed. Ananto had had several urges to listen to the commentary, but he'd been too scared to reach out for the radio.

The man who brought him his lunch at twelve asked after his health and then said, 'Aren't you listening to the commentary, sir? There's a huge crowd around the TV set downstairs.'

'What's the score?'

'Australia's lost four wickets…'

Ananto practically pounced on the radio. They were recapping the morning session before taking listeners back to the studio.

India were all out for 205, Tarsem Kumar being caught at deep point off Lawton off the very third ball of the day. He scored 7. Lawton took 3 for 62, Bright, 2 for 31, Ambrose, 2 for 33, and Leslie, 3 for 50.

At lunch, Australia are on 70 for 4, with Minter batting on 36 and Lawton on 9. Deshraj Anokha has picked up all 4 wickets, bowling an extraordinary spell.

Rogers was the first to go, caught behind the wicket by Shukla off a rising delivery. He had to dive to his left to take a difficult catch. Rogers was on 2 then, with the total at 9. The next batsman to be dismissed was Irwin, for 10, mistiming a hook and giving an easy return catch to Anokha with the total on 16. Woodford was out without scoring, caught by Nabar at short-leg off the third ball he faced, at the same total. Bolan was caught in the slips by Kambatta for 11, when Australia was on 57, after which they added 13 runs without losing any more wickets.

'Get the rest of them quickly, Anokha,' whispered Ananto, 'or I'll die of shame.'

At tea, Australia were 155 for 5, the fifth wicket also having been taken by Anokha. But Minter and Lawton had put on 69 runs before being caught by Kambatta for 47. Lawton was on 64 and Phelps, on 12.

The drama erupted after tea. Mirza had Lawton LBW off the very first ball. One run later, Bright was caught-and-bowled by Patel. Phelps was run out for 17, while Ambrose was bowled by Mirza for a duck. Leslie, the last batsman to be out, was caught by Nabar off Mirza for 5, while Levin remained not out with 17. Australia were bowled out for 183, trailing India by 22 runs. Anokha's figures were 16-2-64-5, Mirza's, 16-4-45-3, and Patel's, 6-1-13-1.

Kambatta changed the batting order in India's second innings, replacing Usmani with himself as the opener, along with Sarin. There was a buzz in the press enclosure. The journalists were preparing to witness the foolishness on Kambatta's part of choosing to face Lawton, Bright and Ambrose with the new ball. One of them said loudly, for everyone's benefit, 'I hope the ambulance is ready. Imagine playing Lawton and Bright at this age.'

Lawton's first ball was a bouncer, a little short of length, rising vertically. Kambatta probably hadn't expected to be greeted this way. Trying to take his head out of the line of the ball, he slipped.

'See what I mean?' a voice in the press enclosure asked jubilantly.

'What's the point of opening the innings when your reflexes are gone?' concurred another journalist in irritation.

'Just watch, Kambatta will try to hit Lawton out of the firing line now,' someone predicted with certainty.

But Kambatta neither attacked any of the bowlers, not went to the hospital. He was not out on 38 at the end of the day, without a single boundary. The three Australian pace bowlers could not penetrate his defence during the twenty-six overs they had bowled collectively between them. Playing steadily and patiently, he took India to 64, but lost three partners in the process.

The first wicket fell at 50, with Sarin at 15. Lawton's delivery stayed very low and trapped him in front of the wicket. After India had added 5 more runs, Ambrose bowled Nabar with the second ball of his over, and had Venkatrangan LBW with his fourth. Nabar had made 3, and Venkatrangan, who was also dismissed off a ball that kept low, did not score. There was just one over to go after Ambrose's, when Usmani went out to bat at number 5. Bending over to take a close look at the pitch, Kambatta said something to Usmani, who took a good look as well.

'There should have been a nightwatchman. Instead of which he sent out a specialist batsman in fading light. What sort of captaincy is this!' Most of the other journalists nodded in agreement.

Usmani pushed the first ball he faced to mid-on for a single. In the next over, the last of the day, he hooked Lawton's bouncer for three. Another bouncer, which Kambatta hooked for 2 runs, was followed by a square-cut off the next ball for two more. He ended the day with a single off a flick to the on side.

India were 86 runs ahead, with 7 wickets in hand,

provided Ananto went out to bat. Twenty-three wickets had fallen in the first two days. In Delhi, 18 wickets had fallen on the very first day, and 25 in the first two. Australia had batted in the fourth innings to win the Test by five wickets—they would have to bat in the fourth innings here as well.

Ananto knocked on Kambatta's door in the evening. 'Yes, come in.'

Panigrahi, the president of the Board, Hariharan, the secretary, Khanna, the manager, and Usmani, the vice-captain, were all present in the room. They looked at him.

'I'll bat tomorrow.'

'It was not your batting but your bowling that I needed, which you could not provide. Thank you for your offer, you don't have to bat.' Kambatta spoke calmly, with pauses.

'You can pack, you'll be put on the plane to Calcutta as soon as the match ends,' Hariharan sounded agitated.

'Even if I can score two runs it will help the team, won't it?' asked Ananto in distress, looking at everyone pleadingly.

'At least ten reporters asked me today after the game why we have a passenger in the team. I didn't tell them I was cheated. I said you fell down in the dressing room and injured yourself after the team was submitted. I had to lie. Yes, the team will gain from two extra runs, but we'd rather play with ten people. I'm sure they can put in a little additional effort to make those two extra runs you have offered so generously.' Kambatta spat his words out, distinctly annoyed at having to speak without wanting to.

'Did you get any phone calls today, Ananto?' Panigrahi asked. Ananto was reeling with anger and humiliation. He shook his head.

'I've left instructions for calls not to be relayed to your room. The press will pounce for news. You will not talk to anyone or meet anyone. You must not even leave your room. We don't want a controversy. Can you ensure that you remember this?' Hariharan was snarling at him.

'You may leave now,' said Panigrahi, pointing to the door. 'Your Test career is over before it could even begin. I feel sorry for you.'

Ananto left the room.

16

But the local newspaper reporters found out from their sources.

'Sen cheats his way into the Test team,' said the *Deccan Herald*.

The Hindu's headline said: 'Was Varde worse?'

'Sen bowls a bouncer to Indian team,' wrote the *Indian Express*.

Putting the newspapers away, Ananto began to brood. Anokha was preparing to go to the stadium. He kept throwing covert glances at Ananto.

'Did you see Jibon yesterday, Anokha?'

'I didn't notice him.'

'Will you tell the manager to send me back to Calcutta on tonight's flight?'

'What do you mean! Aren't you going to bowl in the second innings?'

'They didn't even let me bat...'

'You're able to move around easily. We're definitely

batting through the day. It's the rest day tomorrow. Can't you get yourself fit in two days? Even half-fit will do.'

Ananto smiled. After one, two, three deliveries, it felt like someone was hammering nails into his spine.

'I've told you every single thing they told me. I probably won't be able to bowl even if they ask me to. It's not just the body, the mind and heart must be fit too…Best of luck, Anokha.'

Ananto lay down on his bed and turned on his side. He would sleep now, without even listening to the commentary.

Anokha had said, 'We're definitely batting through the day.' But India's second innings ended on 202 exactly five minutes before tea. Kambatta had scored 94 not out and Usmani, 34. The only other batsman to reach double figures was Durga Das, with 12. Ambrose had taken 4 for 52 from twenty-two overs. Leslie had taken 2 for 9, and Bright, 2 for 21. Lawton bowled twenty-five overs for one wicket, giving away 52 runs, most of them to Kambatta, who could have easily picked up the 6 runs he needed for his century. But he didn't, selflessly giving up countless opportunities for singles to shield the tail-enders. When he was leaving the field, not just the 20,000 spectators present but also the press enclosure gave him a standing ovation.

Australia had to score 225 to win, and they had so much time that no one was thinking about it.

At the end of the third day Australia were 71 for no loss, with Irwin on 53, Rogers on 14, and 4 leg-byes. The wicket was lifeless, but clouds were arriving in the sky. The fourth day of the Test was day after tomorrow. They needed 154 for a win. They would probably get the runs by tea and take a 4-0 lead in the series.

Ananto couldn't bear it in his room anymore. He was not allowed to go out. Returning from the stadium, Anokha lay grimly in his bed for some time. Ananto knew it wasn't right to ask about the game when the team was facing defeat. It would only increase his roommate's discomfort.

But how was he to relieve his own suffering now? How was he to lighten the enormous weight on his chest? Would he have to carry it all his life?

Anokha went out after a shower. He hadn't said a word to Ananto. The doctor had said that the injury would heal not by taking medicines but by keeping his movements to a minimum. Which meant nothing but standing or lying down. Sitting put pressure on his spine, causing pain. Ananto grew furious. He was angry with everyone and everything, most of all with himself. 'Your Test career is over before it could even begin.' Panigrahi's words kept ringing in his ears. All these years of back-breaking work, so many hopes and desires, all dashed to the ground because of one mistake.

As he lay in his bed in the empty room, tears sprang to Ananto's eyes. How was he to atone for this error? Considering how angry Panigrahi and Hariharan were, he was unlikely to get another chance to play for India. At least, not as long as those two were in charge. Newer fast bowlers would appear on the horizon meanwhile. No one would write even a line in his favour in any newspaper. He was finished.

It was the evening of the rest day. Anokha was in someone else's room. The entire team was intimidated by Kambatta's strict instructions. They were forbidden from going outside the hotel or accepting invitations. But there was no restriction on meeting visitors. The key thing was not to allow their physical and mental energies to be dissipated. The match wasn't over yet.

The phone rang.

Ananto got out of bed to answer. It must be for Anokha. He would have to go looking for him.

'Hello.'

'Trunk call from Calcutta for Ananto Sen.'

'Ananto Sen speaking, please connect me.'

He felt a bolt of lightning pass through the length of this body. Who could it be from Calcutta? He couldn't guess.

'Hello, Antu?'

'Ma!'

'I'm at the CAB office. They connected me,' Tonima paused.

'I'm finished, Ma.'

'They're saying you've been injured, Antu.'

'Yes, I slipped in the bathroom…'

'How far did you have to walk to take this call, Antu?'

'Five or six steps.'

'Your legs are fine, then.'

'Why do you say that, Ma?'

'Have you forgotten your father, Antu? Don't you remember anything he said?'

'Yes, I do.'

'Liar.'

Ananto's heart trembled. He had never heard his mother snarl this way.

'Everything they've written about you in the papers today will be forgotten if you remember what your father said, Antu. You have to face his photograph the moment you walk into the house, don't you? As soon as you enter his eyes will ask you, "Why am I not proud of you today, Antu?" How will you answer him, Antu? What will you do? You'll have to steal in through the back door from now on so that you don't have to face your father.'

'No Ma, I can't do that.'

'Are you unhappy with yourself, Antu?'

'I hate myself right now.'

'Then what's the point of this life? What is its value? You won't be able to enjoy anything on earth anymore. You have to rise above this curse, Antu.'

'How, Ma?'

'Do you remember what he had told you that day during the school tournament?' Tonima's voice grew softer, gentler, under the weight of her memories. 'Same ground, same pitch, but you got no wickets in one match, and six in the next. Why? You father had said that unexpected things would be coming your way from now on. Catches would be dropped off your bowling. Dead pitches, poor ground conditions and injuries would not let you bowl naturally. So he had said, "You must overcome all obstacles. You have to prepare yourself in a way that allows you to take wickets even with a broken leg." Have you not prepared yourself that way, Antu? Your leg isn't broken, your hand isn't fractured, is an injury more painful than shattered self-respect?'

'Ma!' Antu whispered. 'They won't let me play in this match anymore.'

'You have to play. You have to bowl. If it kills you, so be it. I will lay down your body in front of your father and tell him, "You had said one say you considered Antu a great man. Look how much greater he has become, your prophecy has come true." Antu... Antu...I'll tell your father, "Look at him, our son..." her voice choked on her tears. The telephone receiver seemed to fall from her hands.

Antu looked around helplessly. Was he still in pain? Did he really have an injury? He ran up to the wall and dashed against it. Where was this injury? He had no pain anywhere, not in his back, not in his hips. Running back to the centre of the room, he threw himself at the wall again and again. What injury? 'No Baba, it's not hurting. See for yourself...see for yourself...see for yourself...'

Like a madman Ananto threw himself at the wall repeatedly, falling back on the floor with a thud each time.

'There's nothing wrong with me, Baba, look, I'm cured.'

He went on shouting. Going up to the window, he screamed at the streetlights, pedestrians and passing traffic, 'I'm feeling well...listen, everyone, I'm feeling well...I'll play, I'll bowl...I'm Ananto...'

Tottering to his bed, he collapsed on it.

17

Climbing into the bus that would take them to the stadium, each of the players paused for a moment on seeing the figure already seated at the back. Ananto was staring out of the window. Kambatta noticed too. His expression became grim.

Ananto was sitting alone in the dressing room. The entire team was on the field, bowling at the nets, practising catches.

One of the stadium employees entered with a cardboard box.

'Someone sent this for you.'

'For me?'

Ananto wondered whether to open it. Best not to. Maybe someone had sent a shoe or a dead rat to insult him. He put the box on the table.

The players were returning to the dressing room, talking amongst themselves, avoiding Ananto. All of them looked intense and determined.

'What's this? Who's this box for?' said Nabar. Removing the lid, he said in surprise, 'Look, a prosthetic arm.'

Ananto jumped up from his chair. 'Mine. It's for me.'

Taking the box from Nabar, he saw a slip of paper inside. It said: 'I don't need this anymore. I'm done playing Tests. Jibon.'

The players were going out for the first session of the day. Ananto was staring at the arm in his lap. He seemed asleep. Suddenly the spell was broken. Ananto ran out. The twelfth man Vinay Marathe was walking down the stairs, behind everyone else. Ananto put his hand on Marathe's shoulder.

'I'm going in, you don't have to go.'

'What! But the captain told me...'

'He made a mistake, I have to bowl today.'

A bewildered Marathe remained standing where he was. Ananto ran into the ground.

Kambatta had reached the pitch. Irwin and Rogers were entering. There were about a thousand spectators, a handful of whom clapped.

Kambatta looked at Ananto in astonishment. 'What are you doing here? Who gave you permission?'

'Let me bowl. Just two overs. I won't ask for more, I'll leave the field.'

Later Kamabatta was to write in his autobiography:

It was a moment that will be etched in my memory

forever. I saw the boy's face. Half god, half demon. I felt a flutter in my heart. What should I do? Give him the ball, or throw him out? I had exactly one second to take a decision. It was probably the most important choice of my life. I gave him the ball. Make your comeback, I said.

I couldn't make out the speed at which he delivered his first ball. I'm told the Pioneer 10 spacecraft which was launched in 1972 is still hurtling through space at 48,000 kilometres per hour. Ananto's ball was probably as fast. Irwin dropped his bat and bent over, clutching his left arm. The ball went into the wicketkeeper's hands off his gloves. The next man in was Woodford. The first ball he faced was an in-swing delivery (remember, the ball was twenty-eight overs old) pitched at his boots. Woodford just stood there, forgetting to lower his bat. One of the bails had to be picked up from where it had landed 30 yards away. Bolan came in to prevent a hat-trick. Ten of us surrounded him. I could clearly see the uncertainty and discomfort in his eyes. He attempted a tentative forward defensive stroke. The ball broke back between the bat and the pad. All of us ran towards Ananto. A hat-trick! Not just the first in Tests for an Indian bowler, but for us, a glimpse of a golden glow of victory on the horizon of defeat.

But Ananto was strangely calm. After the match, he said, not now. From 71 for 0 they were

71 for 3 in just three deliveries. But the wonder was far from over. Ananto's fifth ball landed in my hands via Minter's bat. 71 for 4. At the end of the over Ananto's figures were 1-1-0-4. Even in a hundred years of Test cricket there can't be too many comparable examples of bowling. I saw no sign of any injury-related pain on his face.

Rogers took one run off Mirza's over, and Lawton took two. The fourth ball of Ananto's over was a slower bouncer, following a faster one. Rogers hooked. Venkatrangan showed us what inspired fielding is, running almost forty yards and diving forward to catch the ball flying over his shoulder. Half of Australia were demolished for 74 runs, off 10 deliveries from Ananto.

Even today, when I think of those twelve minutes, I feel we were in the midst of a miracle. The young Bengali seemed to be possessed by a divine force. I still repent my harshness with him over the earlier three days. But then we are flesh-and-blood humans. At that moment, Ananto was not one.

In his fifth over he was on a hat-trick again, having sent Phelps and Bright back with successive rising deliveries on the fourth and fifth balls. Sarin and I took the catches in the slips. Levin appeared on what must have seemed to him like a slaughter-

ground. The bat slipped out of his hands as he walked up to the crease. Ananto's sixth ball thudded onto his back pad. We shouted in appeal. The umpire shook his head, stunning all of us. Even today I am convinced Levin was clearly LBW. The record-books won't show that Ananto got two hat-tricks in an innings, but it will be written in shining letters in my head.

Seven wickets in five overs. Australia were on 85. Ananto had given away all of 6 runs. Usually one batsman puts up some resistance at this stage, which is what Lawton did, playing recklessly. He took 14 off an over from Mirza, and 8 off Ananto. Levin got out to Mirza without scoring, scooping an easy return catch probably just to ensure he didn't have to face Ananto.

After this, it was just a matter of time. It came four overs later, as Ananto picked up his ninth scalp, getting Leslie out leg before the wicket. The umpire was the same gentleman who had deprived him of his hat-trick. Lawton remained not out on 39. Australia batted for exactly an hour on the fourth day, adding 60 runs. Their innings ended on 131, and they lost by 93 runs. Ananto's figures: 12-7-21-9.

This account will remain incomplete without

describing a strange scene in the dressing room. It took time for the expected joy to erupt after the match. The entire stadium was overwhelmed by this unbelievable bowling display. I saw tears in every Indian player's eyes. In spectators' eyes too. But Ananto was steady, unmoved, humble. Scooping a little soil off the pitch, he looked up at the sky, muttered something, and put in his pocket. That was the only time I saw a trace of emotion on his face. Before walking off the ground he told me, 'Thank you for giving me a chance today, sir.' I tried to look serious, saying, 'Don't lie ever again.' But in my head I said, I have no doubt of your integrity, Ananto, or you would not have exploded this way. I will be forever grateful to you for the honour you gave me as a gift, in the twilight of my cricketing career. I had not imagined winning this Test when we walked on to the field.

And then came the scene in the dressing room. Anokha dragged a young man into our presence, his right arm amputated from the wrist downwards. He had been sitting quietly somewhere. A friend of Ananto's. Anokha screamed, 'Here's the root cause of all the trouble. He's the one who instigated Sen today.' Then Ananto and his friend began to talk to each other in Bangla. Since I do not know the *language, I cannot recount what they told each other.*

'Give my arm back Antu, put it back in place.'

'I won't. You'll only hit me with it. Promise you won't?'

'I won't.'

Ananto held his right hand out. 'Here's your arm back.'